INSATIABLE GHOST MONSTER

GALLICHAN MANOR BOOK 1

KHLOE WREN

ISBN ebook: 978-0-6451747-5-5
ISBN print: 978-0-6451747-6-2

Copyright © Khloe Wren 2022

Cover Credits:
Digital Artist: Khloe Wren

Editing Credits:
Editor: Carolyn Depew of Write Right Edits

No AI was used to create this cover or story

CHAPTER
ONE

LISA

JOGGING UP THE STEPS, I rushed to get out of the downpour. My current home was a crappy apartment that was only a small step up from being homeless, but it had a roof that didn't leak, the rent was cheap, and it was safer than being out in the open. Although, if I couldn't find a job in the next week, I wouldn't even be able to afford this place.

Wiping the rain from my face, I didn't linger in the entryway. I'd seen all sorts of shit go down here that I'd rather not be part of. Within minutes, I was up the stairs and unlocking my door. Once closed inside, I flipped the deadbolt, slid the chain-lock into place, then did a quick check of my sparse, one-bedroom unit in case anyone had broken in while I was out at another failed job interview.

Turned out being an excellent librarian wasn't a very marketable skill set outside of libraries. It also didn't help that I'd had to leave my last few positions suddenly without any notice, so I had no references even if I could find a library anywhere near Baltimore that was currently hiring.

Once I was sure I was alone and safe, I dumped my bag on the kitchen counter then went to grab the envelope from the floor near the door. I hadn't thought there was enough of a gap under the thing to shove anything through, but clearly, I'd been wrong. Nerves had my fingers trembling as I picked it up, dreading who it might be from.

I prayed it was anything but a note from my stalker. My finances couldn't take another move. Not yet. I'd had nearly a year in Washington before he'd found me. Stupidly, I'd settled in, started to make a life for myself there, thinking he'd given up and moved on. But then one morning I'd turned up at the Washington Public Library for my shift and there he was, sitting at the tables, reading like he had every right to be there.

Anger mixed with my nerves at the memory of all I'd been forced to leave behind two months ago. I'd had a nice apartment, loved my job, even started making friends with a couple of the other single ladies who'd lived in my apartment building. I hadn't worked up the courage to try to date yet, but it no longer seemed impossible. My drawer full of toys helped take the edge off, but they weren't the same as the warm flesh of a real man.

But as always, my past caught up with me and it became necessary to run. When I'd initially fled Washington, I'd been heading to New York City, figuring it would be easy to get lost in a city that size, but my car had other plans. When the old clunker broke down just outside of Baltimore, I knew it was dead for good.

Using my phone, I searched for a junkyard close by. Going with the first one I found, I called and arranged for them to come collect both me and the vehicle. After arriving back at their yard, I'd happily sold them my car for cash. The only thing I'd taken before I fled Washington had been my go-bag, so with that and the cash, I'd left the yard and went looking for accommodations and found this place where I could lay low until I could work out what the hell I should do next.

I jumped at the sound of a door slamming closed and winced when less than a minute later, the deep thump of bass from my neighbor's stereo vibrated through me. With a sigh in anticipation of the headache I'd soon have, I ripped open the envelope and pulled free the letter, wanting to get it over with. If he'd found me, I'd just have to hitchhike to New York.

The paper was thick, much thicker than the standard stuff most people ran through their printers. Hopefully that meant it wasn't my stalker. I unfolded the letter and sighed in relief when I confirmed it wasn't from him.

At the top of the page there was a fancy round logo featuring a building that looked a little like the White House, with the words "Gallichan Manor" in a classic block font underneath, then a few paragraphs of flowing cursive handwriting in the center of the page, which reminded me of my past. The last foster home I was in before aging out of the system was owned by an older lady who'd refused to accept modern technology. She'd rejected using a mobile phone or computer, wrote everything out in cursive and if I didn't want to get into trouble for not properly doing the grocery shopping, I had to figure out how to read her handwriting correctly. As much as I'd hated it as a teen, it was a skill I'd put to good use over my years of working in libraries.

Heading into the kitchen, I pulled out a glass and filled it with water before moving to sit on the lone chair that sat at the table so I could focus fully on reading exactly what had been written. Finally finished, I sat back in shock. This seemed too good to be true. The owners of Gallichan Manor wanted their private library cataloged and sorted. I would reside at the manor with all living expenses covered until the job was completed, at which time I'd be paid $100,000. The job was anticipated to take at least three months. The offer was pure insanity. The best I'd ever earned as a librarian was about half that amount per year.

Draining my glass of water, I went back to refill it as I mulled over the offer. Something that sounded this good was surely some kind of con, right? My thoughts were cut off when my other neighbors arrived home already fighting, the woman screaming at her man loud enough I could hear it over the music still blaring through from the first neighbor to arrive home. Shivers ran down my spine and with a glance around at my meager belongings and the crappy furniture that had come with the place, I decided wherever this manor was, it had to be better than here. Especially if I got to work with books. I doubted I'd actually get that payout at the end, but if my living expenses were covered, I could deal with that for payment. I hoped it was out of town, far enough away from anywhere my stalker would be currently searching for me.

Returning to the table, I re-read the instructions on how to accept the offer, then pulled out my phone and tapped out a text to the number listed, accepting the job. Before I had time to set my phone down, it dinged with a response. Nerves once more had my fingers trembling as I opened the text.

A car will be in front of your apartment building in twenty minutes to pick you up.

Blowing out a breath, I tucked my phone in my pocket and set about packing my few possessions. Since I'd had a job interview today, I was already wearing the one half-decent outfit I owned, a pencil skirt and fitted, button up shirt. Perfect for a librarian, not so much for the waitress job interview I'd had today. But without a job, I'd had to make do with the few things I'd had in my go-bag on top of what I'd been wearing when I'd left.

Once I was packed and ready to go, I sent a text to my landlord, who wrote back telling me to leave my keys on the kitchen counter and to not even think about asking for a refund for the rest of the month I'd already paid for. That wasn't surprising, since he'd seemed like a typical slum landlord when I first rented the place.

Then I was heading out the door for the last time while praying this job was the real deal and not some elaborate hoax my stalker had set up to get hold of me.

Exactly twenty minutes after I'd received the text, my mouth went dry at the sleek, black Mercedes Benz that pulled up in front of me. I'd been waiting in the shadows, out of the rain, under the eaves of the apartment building and was still in shock for a few moments. It had to be brand new, and it stuck out like a sore thumb in this shitty neighborhood. As soon as it stopped, I snapped out of my stupor and rushed from my hiding spot toward the vehicle. The last thing I needed was for the driver to get carjacked, which would no doubt be the end of the job – and escape – I desperately needed.

A well-dressed man who I guessed was in his fifties, came around to open the rear door for me.

"Miss Smith, if you'd be so kind as to settle yourself quickly, we'll be on our way."

His gaze flicked to a few of the deeper shadows down the street, as though he'd had the same thought as I just had.

"Is this all your luggage, ma'am?"

Heat flared over my cheeks. "Um, yeah. That's it."

Acting like he didn't notice my embarrassment, he took my bag from me as I climbed in, and after closing my door, he made fast work of putting my stuff in the trunk before going around to the driver's door. I'd barely gotten my seatbelt clicked in place when the car smoothly glided away from the curb. Leaning forward, I cleared my throat.

"The letter didn't say where Gallichan Manor is located. Is it far?"

He smiled gently into the mirror as his gaze locked with mine for a moment before returning to the road, "It's located on the outskirts of the Wharton State Forest, near Hammonton in New Jersey. We have a few hours' drive ahead of us. Plenty of time if you'd like to have a nap before your arrival."

Relief poured through me that we were traveling so far. Since the sun was just setting, I figured it would be near midnight before we arrived at the manor. Feeling more relaxed, but not at all sleepy, I decided to attempt to chat with the man who was going to be my only company for the evening.

"Thanks. What's your name? Do you live at the manor too?"

"My name is Henry, ma'am, and yes, I live and work at the manor. I'll put up the screen, so you're not woken by the oncoming traffic as we drive."

Before I could think of a response to his strangely friendly yet abrupt comment, a black screen rose up, sealing me alone in the rear of the vehicle. I frowned at it for a few moments, replaying that whole strange conversation. A tendril of fear trickled down my spine as I started to feel woozy. I reached for the door, wanting to open the window, but I'd barely managed to lift my arm before I was drifting into unconsciousness.

NOAH

Miss Smith certainly was a pretty little thing. She was tall for a human, but compared to my seven feet, two-inch height, she was small. Dark, almost black hair, cut off in a straight line just above her shoulders in such a way I suspected she'd done it herself. Black-rimmed glasses framed her thickly lashed eyes. Her face was a masterpiece of delicate features I couldn't wait to become familiar with. With a grin, I shifted to hover in front of her. Now she'd succumbed to the gas, I didn't need to wait any longer.

In my ghost form, the gas canister I'd released after Henry had sealed us in didn't affect me, and I couldn't be seen or felt. That is, unless I wanted to be, and I most definitely wanted her to feel me. With the lightest of touches, I stroked a fingertip down her nose, the softness of her skin sending a shiver down my spine that had my tail twitching. Licking my own lips, I traced her lower one with my thumb until her mouth opened enough for me to slide the digit within. Her tongue was warm against my skin, and I leaned closer to whisper a command into her ear.

"Suck like you would a cock."

Few could resist the allure of a ghost's voice, and my sweet little Lisa was thankfully not one of those few. Her lips tightened around me as she began to alternate between running her tongue over my flesh and sucking it deep into her mouth. Oh, I couldn't wait until later when I could get my cock down her throat. It was big and would stretch her lips wide, and the anticipation of watching her struggle to take me had my cock twitching.

Another shudder ran through me as I lowered my gaze to her chest. With the back of my free hand, I rubbed over her nipples until they were hard points against the thin fabric of her blouse. As she continued to suck my thumb like a pro, I unclicked her seatbelt before slipping the buttons free and parting the pale pink material to reveal which of her collection of sexy underwear she was wearing. The lacy, lavender bra was more sedate than I'd been expecting to find her wearing, but the way her dark nipples poked at the lace, begging for some attention, was perfection. Who was I to neglect such a demand?

Pulling the lacy fabric down under each of her tits, I took in the sight she made. On the outside, sweet Miss Smith was a lady, always wearing prim skirts and blouses. She was someone my mother would have no doubt approved of and welcomed into the family. But I was more interested in what lay beneath her surface.

The moment I first saw her six months ago in the Washington library, she'd caught my attention. Dressed so prim and proper, I needed to know what lay beneath. So, using my ghost form, I'd followed her home and set about learning all I could about her. I'd quickly worked out that underneath that sweet exterior lay a sexual woman with needs I was perfectly equipped to sate.

In my long life, I'd never seen so many adult toys outside of a sex shop as I had the first time I'd slipped into her bedroom at night. I'd struggled to not help her get off when I caught her fucking herself with a dildo nearly as big as I was. She'd rammed that thing in nice and deep with every stroke, seeming to enjoy the bite of pain it mixed in with her pleasure. That was definitely something I would gladly help her with, over and over again.

But then she'd up and vanished, leaving everything behind except her car, while I'd made a trip back to the manor to check on things. It'd taken me months to track down where she'd gone. I had no clue why she'd left her comfortable home and life to move to the shitty apartment I found her in, but I couldn't leave her there unguarded. Not when I sensed danger was closing in on her.

She scraped her teeth over my thumb and pulled my mind back to her in the present. My cock throbbed as I took in the way her tits were framed by her bra, poking out toward me, begging for attention. Her cheeks hollowed as she sucked my thumb and there was a shine of saliva over her chin. Fuck, she was a wet dream come true. Well, nearly. If I could get her skirt and panties off her, then she'd truly be a dream-worthy image.

Leaving her tits for the moment and sliding my thumb free from her mouth, I moved to gather her skirt up around her waist. It took a little wriggling to get the fitted pencil skirt up under her ass, but I soon managed and was rewarded with the sight of a pair of lacy panties that matched the bra. Taking a deep inhale near her pussy, I grinned as the scent of her arousal filled my senses.

Gripping either side of her panties, I

pulled them down her curvy hips and legs. Once off, I tossed them aside and after nudging her knees as wide as she could sit, floated back again to take in the sight she made.

She was one hundred percent good girl gone bad in this moment. If I could, I'd take a photo. I turned to the partition that separated us from Henry, the family's trusted butler and driver. I'd never bothered to keep up with technology, had no need for it, but I did know that Henry had one of those fancy phones that could take photos. I could ask him to take one for me…

I shook my head. No. I wouldn't risk him inhaling the last of the gas in the vehicle. And what would I do with a photo? Better to enjoy my new toy and store every moment away in my memory, where only I could see them.

Moving my focus back to Lisa, I decided she was too much of a temptation and I wasn't going to wait until later to get my first taste of her and her skills. Floating up before her face, I took my erect cock into my hand and rubbed the tip over her lower lip, spreading some precum there.

"Open wide and suck my cock deep. Show me how good you can deep throat."

Like the good girl she was, she opened her mouth and I slid in, stretching her lips wide as I went deep before I began to thrust in and out. She gagged the first time but then without me needing to tell her, breathed through her nose and swallowed against me the next time I hit the back of her throat. My eyes crossed at how good she felt around me when she started to hum.

Lengthening my tail, I slid it up the inside of her thigh until it found the slick heat it was searching for. Delving between her folds, I mimicked my tail thrusts with my cock, fucking both her pussy and mouth at the same time.

"Get your hands on your tits, and pinch and twist your nipples until they ache."

Like a well-trained pet, she followed my orders and began to torment her tight little buds as I continued to pump her throat and pussy. Fuck, she was Nirvana and I never wanted it to stop. After a few minutes of her roughly playing with her tits, she began to moan, the sound causing her throat to vibrate around me until I couldn't stop from coming.

I might be in my ghost form, but I was still male enough to have plenty of cum to give to my woman. Later, I would definitely be filling up her pretty little pussy with a whole lot of my seed. Since I hadn't mated her, pregnancy wasn't a concern, and I couldn't catch any diseases she may carry so I could come inside her all I wanted.

"Swallow down every drop. It's a gift and not a drop is to be wasted."

With another groan, she roughly twisted her nipples at my words. Hmm, seemed my little pet liked some dirty talk to go with her bite of pain. I could give her both, no trouble. Then all thoughts ended as I emptied myself down her throat, loving how she struggled to swallow it all. When my mind returned to being functional, I pulled my still hard cock from her mouth but held it in front of her as she automatically licked me clean.

"Such a good girl. I think you've earned a reward."

When I slipped my tail free, she whined and squirmed in the seat as she rolled her nipples between her thumbs and forefingers. I grinned as I moved down. Her tits were going to ache for days after the way she was treating them. I couldn't wait to watch her squirm.

Once my face was between her creamy-white thighs, I pulled her forward on the seat, so her pussy landed against my mouth. After giving her clit a rough tug and nip, I thrust my tongue in deep, allowing it to grow thicker and longer until it filled her channel completely before I started tongue fucking her.

Reaching up, I brushed her hands away and took over playing with her nipples, alternating tender strokes with rough tugs and twists. It didn't take long before she was panting, and her body tensed. Knowing she was close, I gave each nipple a rough, hard twist at the same time as I nipped her clit and she screamed and came. I sucked down every drop of nectar she gave me, unable to get enough. I kept at her until she came twice more, deciding right then that I could live solely on her cream. When she began to whimper and thrash her head from side to side, I knew my time was nearly up. The effects of the gas were wearing off.

Reluctantly, I pulled free from her lush body and returned all her clothing to its original placement along with her seatbelt. It was such a pity to cover up such beauty, but I was quite sure I'd have her naked and at my mercy again before the sun rose.

TWO

LISA

I woke slightly groggy as the car rolled up a long, gravel driveway. For some reason, my nipples ached to the point of pain and my jaw was tight. There was also an odd pressure between my legs. I looked down at myself, relieved to see all my clothing was securely in place. As I'd slept, I had the most erotic dream of my entire life, and I could only guess the tightness in my body was nothing more than residual effects of the dream. Taking my glasses off, I scrubbed my hands over my face before putting them back on and looking out the window to see the front of a mansion lit by moonlight.

"Oh, my!"

What I assumed was the Gallichan Manor looked like it was a close relative of the White House. Tall columns lined the front of the huge, stone structure. Clearly, this was the building from the logo on the letter I'd received. The car glided to a stop and in shock, I didn't move until Henry opened the door and the cool breeze from outside hit my face, waking me from my stupor. I stumbled as I exited the car, my gaze still caught on the size of the place.

"This way, Miss Smith. I'll show you to your rooms, then in the morning, I'll show you the library and other common rooms. I'll also explain the specifics of your job."

I nodded, struggling to form words as I followed him toward the front door. Once inside, I stopped for a moment to take in the dimly lit foyer. Even with the dull lighting, it was clearly a stunning space.

"You'll have plenty of time in the morning to explore. For now, it's late and time to turn in for the evening. You'll find a tray of food in your rooms. You also have a full bathroom, complete with a large tub. You are welcome to use anything within your suite of rooms, but please don't leave them until I've been able to show you the rest of the house. It's easy to get lost, especially in the evening. And the owners of the house prefer low lighting, so it's rather dark at night."

Forcing my legs to keep moving, I followed closely behind Henry as he moved confidently through the dimly lit space. After opening a door, he moved to set my bag on the floor beside a four-poster king size bed. My gaze was stuck on that enormous mattress. I could happily live on that thing. It was like something out of a fairytale.

"Here you go. You'll find clothing and toiletries already in the closets. The master was confident of you accepting his invitation."

I nodded, only half hearing him and then he was gone, the door shutting behind him with a solid thunk. The smell of something delicious drew me over to a sitting area where an old-school hotel food trolley sat with a few silver domes on it. After lifting the lids, I nearly fell into a heap on the floor, shock weakening my knees before I could slump into a seat.

Even when I'd had a job, my budget

never included being able to eat like this. One plate held what looked to be some sort of seafood risotto, the shrimp delicately placed on the top of the dish were the biggest I'd ever seen. Another plate held a roasted chicken breast, with red sauce artfully dribbled over it and a yellow cake type thing next to it. No idea what that was, but all together it smelled delicious. The third plate held a juicy looking steak, with steamed vegetables perfectly placed beside it. A small gravy boat sat beside that plate. There were two bottles of wine, a red and a white, along with a tall glass bottle of chilled water, if the condensation on the outside of it was any indication. Dessert was yet another plate filled with several small ball-type things that I'm sure would be delicious.

Removing my glasses, I once more rubbed my palms over my face as I struggled to believe all this was real. Was I still in the car asleep? I lowered my hands, returned my glasses, and pinched myself on the tender skin of my inner upper arm. When the pain flared but nothing changed, I shook my head.

"This is actually real. Damn."

Lifting the cutlery, I pulled forward the steak. With my mouth watering, I sliced off a corner, but when the bloody interior was revealed, I shuddered and quickly pushed that plate away and returned the dome lid. I liked my meat dead, not still running around my plate. That steak looked like it only saw the flame as it went past, rather than being cooked over it.

Thankfully, the chicken was cooked to perfection, and I devoured half before pushing it aside to try the seafood dish. I ate until I was stuffed fuller than I could ever remember being and with a sigh, sat back with the glass of white wine I'd poured myself to sip at while looking around the room. Across from the bed was an open fireplace that had a fire crackling away within its hearth, with several logs neatly stacked beside it and I made a mental note to remember to add a few before I went to sleep.

As I sat in the comfortable chair, I reached over for one of the little dessert balls and within moments of popping it in my mouth groaned in bliss. Chocolate and cherry goodness flooded my mouth and my eyes rolled back at the pleasure the flavor brought me. Despite being overly full, I still reached for a second one, a white chocolate and raspberry flavor that also left me moaning. My nipples tingled and a shudder ran through me as I swallowed the last of it.

I frowned down at the front of my blouse to see my nipples were hard little points, poking against my shirt. That was odd. Another tingle ran through each as though something had brushed over them, but there was nothing anywhere near them other than my shirt.

Figuring it was another remnant from my earlier erotic dream, I stood and made my way over to what I hoped would be the bathroom. Passing under an open archway, I flipped the switch on the wall and dull light filled the space, confirming I'd guessed correctly. This room was the most luxurious bathroom I'd ever seen. A deep tub was featured in the center like it was the showpiece of the room. Going over to it, I blew out a low breath. A dozen jets were around the sides, and built-in pillows at the top and bottom made it clear it was designed for a couple. A pang hit my heart and I rubbed a fist between my breasts.

I was a nobody foster kid all grown up. Happily ever afters with a man weren't in my future. I'd tried to live the dream once and all I'd gotten in the end was a stalker. Moving over to the sink, I opened drawers to discover that just as Henry had said, it was fully stocked with everything I could need.

All the delicious, rich food I'd eaten was making me sleepy, so I decided to try out the bath another day. I grabbed what I'd need for a shower and placed the bottles in the alcove of the huge, enclosed area before I set a big, fluffy towel on the vanity counter near the shower. Then I flipped the taps on to heat while I stripped out of my clothes. Leaving them in a neat pile on the counter, I stepped into the shower and after adjusting the temperature, moved under the water that felt like rain as it tumbled down from the large showerhead. Oh, I could definitely get used to this place. Great food and awesome facilities. I couldn't wait to see what books the library contained.

Grabbing the shampoo, I lathered up and as I leaned back to rinse, there was a tug on my right nipple. Swiping the water from my face, I looked down but there was nothing there. While I was watching, my left nipple was tugged, then both were on fire and before my eyes, my breasts pulled out as though someone was playing with the tips.

As quickly as it happened, it stopped, and I blinked a few times as I cupped my breasts, running my palms over my hard — sore — nipples.

"That was odd."

With a shake of my head, I finished washing my hair, then conditioned it, something I hadn't had the luxury of affording in over a month.

"Put your hands against the tile and spread your feet as wide as you can."

The silky voice came out of nowhere but it was familiar, possibly from my earlier dream. Yes. It had been in my dream. Maybe I'd already gone to bed and fallen asleep? In my dream, I'd gotten immense pleasure when listening to that voice, so that's what I did now because I wanted more of that. Turning, I pressed my palms against the cold tile and moved my feet to a wider stance.

"Good girl. So pretty, all wet for me."

My sore nipples were again on fire as though rough fingers twisted and tugged on them. My core clenched with need, and I whimpered out a plea. "Please."

Then heat fanned across my pussy a moment before something pressed in deeply. Arousal coursed through my body, but I managed to force my gaze downward and saw nothing but air. Confusion warped my mind for a moment, then I felt something slip down between my butt cheeks and settle over my ass hole and I flinched forward. I'd been forced to leave my toys behind when I'd fled Washington, and I'd never felt adequately safe at my crappy apartment to lower my guard enough to allow myself to feel any sort of arousal. After not touching myself in two months, my body was strung tightly, desperate for release.

Teeth nipped at my clit, and I sucked in a breath as a shudder ran through me.

"You will hold still and let me explore all your holes. They are all mine to use as I wish."

Before my mind could catch up with my body, I was nodding and relaxing into the touch when it returned to my rear entrance, rubbing in gentle circles before slipping inside me. My body was on fire and my thoughts tripped over each other as something thick, slick and hot thrust in and out of my pussy at a rapid pace while what felt like a finger fucked my ass. I moaned when a second digit joined the first, stretching my back entrance wider. My hips rocked between the two invasions, seeking more from both sides. A deep chuckle echoed around the shower stall as a third finger entered my ass and whatever was fucking my pussy grew wider, stretching me there too. A harsh pinch to my clit had me screaming as I came with a violent tremor.

When my thoughts cleared, I found myself curled on the tile floor, panting and still shaking with aftershocks of the most intense orgasm I'd ever experienced. It was another few minutes before I could muster the energy to stand and finish rinsing out the conditioner, then gently wash my sensitive body.

Was my imagination really that expressive? To give me a waking dream that left me coming so hard I saw stars? It was the only thing that made any sort of sense. Turning off the shower, I dried quickly and with just the towel wrapped around my body, I made my way to the large bed. After the food and now the orgasm, I was too tired to bother finding pajamas, so after draping the towel over the back of a nearby chair, I slipped naked between the sheets where sleep quickly overtook me.

NOAH

Taking in how she looked like a broken doll lying there panting under the cascading water on the floor had precum seeping from my cock. I needed to fuck all her holes. Fill her up every way I could, as often as I could.

She was perfect.

I didn't touch her as she rose to finish her shower and dry off, but I stroked my cock the whole time. Especially when she climbed into the bed naked. As she slipped into sleep, I added more logs to the fire to keep the room warm, then headed over to the trolley where I switched to my monster form and finished off the food she'd left and drank a glass of red wine as I waited for my new little toy to be fully asleep so I could have some more fun.

Having her in a sexual haze by the time she arrived at my library in the morning was my goal. I couldn't wait to see her reaction to what the section of the library where I'd have her begin was stocked with. Tomorrow night was one I'd been anticipating for a long time, ever since I'd seen Lisa in the library when I'd gone in to acquire books for the tamer portion of my collection. I'd kept tabs on her since then, monitoring what she was up to, who she was seeing. Which wasn't hard, considering she mostly kept to herself. She'd seemed to be opening up to those around her when she'd vanished. The way she'd left everything behind had me wondering if someone had threatened her and she'd run.

The anger that had risen within me at that thought made it clear this woman was destined to be mine. I'd never felt this need to protect and possess before Lisa. Once I'd located her again and discovered her living in that horrible little apartment, I knew I had to save her. Human predators were watching her, stalking what was mine. It had been necessary to dispatch one just the other day.

I'd been grateful when she'd failed at another job interview and became desperate enough that she'd accept the offer I put forward. I knew if it was made too early, she'd have rejected it, so I stayed in the shadows, guarding her until I believed she'd reached the point where she would take the risk.

Timing was critical with these things, and I'd timed it perfectly because she was now in my bed and was ripe for the picking. Speaking of picking…

Taking my ghost form again, I moved to hover over her sleeping body, watching her looking so peaceful for a few moments before I gently peeled the covers back to reveal all her curves. She'd lost weight since I'd first seen her, a natural side-effect of the financial hardship she found herself in, but I'd get her back to her previous, lush perfection soon. She'd eaten much of the food I had the chef prepare for her, so I was certain she'd have plenty of energy to keep up with me tonight.

Gently rolling her onto her back, I moved her legs wide before kneeling between them. Then I returned to my monster form, so she'd be able to see me and what I was doing to her if she woke. No doubt, she'd continue to believe she was dreaming, but I wanted her to see me take her the first time I got my cock up her pussy and inside that tight ass of hers.

In my monster form, my blood ran hot, and soon the room became warm enough she began to shift and wake. Lowering down, I licked at her nipple, knowing they were no doubt extremely sensitive by now. I didn't do more than lick at each one as I wrapped my fingers around her hips. With a groan, she blinked her eyes open and jerked when she saw me, which was a fair reaction. I was seven feet, two inches of red-skinned, muscular monster. Dark ram horns curled around either temple, standing out starkly against my long pale red hair and my black eyes could mesmerize just like my voice when I was in ghost form.

"Who- What are you?"

"Your dream come true. A monster of your very own to protect you and lavish you with attention and affection." I smirked down at her, licking my tongue over my dark red lips. "And sex. There will be lots of fucking."

Before she could respond, I leaned down and nibbled at her nipple, taking the hard tip between my teeth and pulling up until the skin was taut and she arched her back on a gasp. Releasing her, I lifted my hand to the other breast, twisting the nipple roughly before tugging that one in the same manner as I'd done with my mouth on the first. I wound my tail around until it could tease her clit before slipping down to her opening, where it thrust in deep, not stopping until I bottomed out. She shuddered and tensed when I tapped her cervix.

"You like some pain with your pleasure, *mascota*. That's convenient because I like to deliver just that."

I continued tormenting her nipples until they were as dark red as my lips, and diamond-hard as they responded to my touch. I thickened my tail, sending pulses through the length. Her eyes opened wide, and she reached up and, after running her fingers into my hair, gripped my horns. A shudder ran through me at the contact. A monster's horns were almost as sensitive as his cock when aroused. With a growl that shook the painting above the bed, I pulled my tail free and lined my thick erection up with her hole.

"Watch me claim you, *mascota*."

After moving her legs to my shoulders, I shifted my hands to under her ass, lifting her pelvis so she could easily see when I lined up and slowly breached her tight opening with my monster dick. Her eyes were wide and her mouth open as her gaze stayed glued to where I was joining us. Tears pooled in her eyes, but arousal flushed her cheeks, neck and chest. I was certain she felt the burn as she stretched to take my wide girth. She hadn't taken any of her toys with her when she'd run, so it'd been months since she'd stretched her pussy out with a dildo. I was bigger than the plastic cocks she'd been fucking herself with, but I knew she wouldn't complain. A little pain was right up her alley.

"Get your hands on your tits. Roll those

tight, little buds. Tug and twist them. Torture yourself for me, *mascota*."

Calling her pet in my native language felt right. She was my pretty little pet who I'd treat like a queen out in the world but in here, she'd be my dirty little pet. Here for my pleasure, and hers. I'd always make sure she got hers because watching her get off was part of the high for me.

I bottomed out, my cock head up against her cervix. I grinned at the way she tensed and shuddered while she moaned.

"You like that? Having your cervix tapped?" I thrust out and in again to demonstrate, and her eyes nearly rolled back in her head as her hands held her breasts firmly.

"Don't stop torturing those nipples, I want to see how red you can make them while I own this pussy. Then once I get done here, I'm gonna take that pretty little ass. It's been a long time since you've had a cock up there, hasn't it? And never one as big as mine."

She grunted an affirmative noise. I'd tease her about her toy collection, but I didn't want to scare her off with how long

I'd been watching her just yet. With a wide grin, I pulled out and thrust in once more. "You'll love it. I'll get my whole length inside you that way. I can't fucking wait, but first, gotta break in this pussy. Give those tits a hard twist for me, *mascota*. Yeah, that's it. Again."

She wouldn't be able to stand the feel of a bra on her skin tomorrow and I couldn't fucking wait. I picked up my pace, thrusting in as deeply as I could go, making sure to nudge her cervix, then glide over her g-spot on the withdrawal of every stroke. Within minutes, she was thrashing against me, begging me for more. I doubted she knew what it was she wanted more of, but I'd give it to her. So much fucking more. Probably more than she could handle, but hopefully she'd find a way, because I wasn't going to be done with her for a good long while. If ever.

THREE

LISA

A HUGE, long haired, red monster with horns was fucking me senseless. His enormous dick was only three quarters of the way in, but the tip tapped my cervix on every stroke, the stab of pain blending with the pleasure of him gliding over my g-spot on every stroke. My fingers stayed on my nipples, twisting and tugging as his gaze watched. They hurt, the ache rapidly blurring into pain, but I couldn't stop, couldn't refuse his order.

Then he gripped my ankles and after putting them together in front of him, rolled my lower half to the side, changing the angle of his penetration as he kept fucking me.

"Oh fuck…"

I didn't normally curse but this position made the fit tighter and I could feel every ridge and dip of his huge cock as it continued to fuck me. Releasing my breasts, I reached out and took fists full of the sheets as I came. Stars filled my vision as he continued to pound into me, extending the orgasm until I could barely breathe. Then with a growl, he came, hot jets filling my womb. His climax went on forever, and I was sure he'd completely filled my uterus with his cum. Could he get me pregnant?

Before I could voice my question, he rolled me the rest of the way over and pulled my cheeks apart. I turned as he lowered and lapped his long, thick tongue over my rear hole. It'd been five years since a man had fucked my ass. It was that act that had turned my ex from lover to owner. He'd taken my dark needs and twisted them into something they weren't. Claiming I liked being used and abused, he'd started pimping me out to the roughest of his friends.

Once I'd gotten away from him, I'd

never risked letting a man get that close again. Toys were all I allowed myself. But this monster pushed all those doubts away without hesitation. I wanted him inside me. Wanted this beast to claim me fully with his carnal delights.

Reaching under me, he delved three fingers into my pussy and scooped out some cum that he then used to lube up my ass, repeating what I thought I'd imagined in the shower. He worked me up till he had three fingers pumping in that forbidden hole. I wanted to ask about the shower, but the pleasure/pain sparks he was creating were too much to even think of speaking through. He slipped a fourth finger in and after a few more pumps, withdrew them and lined his dick up with my now stretched hole.

He paused and looked up to see me watching him.

"Look in the mirror and watch me claim your ass."

My gaze flipped around the room, landing on the huge mirror hanging on the wall beside the bed. How had I not noticed that earlier?

I took in my body, my nipples nearly as

deep red as his lips, arousal making my eyes bright, and cheeks flushed. My chest was also red with a flush.

A sharp sting on my butt had my gaze swinging to him.

"Watch me fuck your ass, *mascota*. You can look at how pretty you are all mussed up later."

Once my gaze caught on his long, thick cock, I couldn't look away. He held my cheek out with one hand and used the other to press the head against my hole. Just like with my pussy, he used a slow, steady pace to press inside me. But unlike my pussy, there was nothing to stop him from pushing his full length inside my back entrance. Once he was fully seated, his heavy balls slapping against my wet pussy, I could barely breathe, stretched to the point I wondered if I was about to be torn in two. None of my toys had ever been this big. Squeezing my eyes closed, I waited for the pain to ease. Another sharp sting had my eyes opening to see he'd spanked me again.

"Eyes open."

With a hand around each of my hips, he moved me until I was up on my hands and knees, then he pulled out nearly all the way. A bottle of lube was in his hand—where it came from, I had no clue— but he glided easily into me after he squirted the cool liquid over his cock, something for which I was grateful. After several thrusts, he ran a palm up between my breasts and lifted my shoulders until my back was against his chest. I wrapped my hands around his horns, needing to hold onto something. As soon as I wrapped my fingers around them, he shuddered and thrust deeper. Then his hands were on my poor, abused breasts and he began to torture my nipples once more.

"No bra tomorrow. I want you unbound all day."

I shook my head. Despite dropping some weight lately, I was still an E cup, way too large to be going braless.

He brutally twisted them both. "You will give me what I want within these walls, *mascota*. No bra or panties tomorrow. I will be watching you all day. I want to know I can have easy access, so that means a skirt or dress, and no underwear."

The glide in and out of my ass was such a different sensation, one that had arousal pounding through my body like I'd never experienced. I knew I'd pass out soon from the overload of sensations.

"It was you in the shower, wasn't it?"

He lowered his mouth to my shoulder where he sunk his teeth into the flesh, breaking the skin before he licked the blood away.

"Yes, *mascota*. It was also me in the car. In my ghost form, I can have you whenever — wherever — I want."

Before I could respond, another climax rose up and crashed over me, taking my ability to think with it. I was barely able to focus to hear his roar and feel the hot splash of his seed filling up my ass. If it was him in the car and not a dream, he'd now filled my belly, pussy and ass with his seed tonight.

Add in the bite mark he'd left on my shoulder just now, and I was well and truly marked by this monster.

NOAH

Back in my ghost form, I stayed close to her the following morning. She hesitated over her underwear. I'd only included a few bras and panties when I'd stocked the closet for her, figuring she'd appreciate them when she needed to leave the house, but she wouldn't need them for when she was here. She normally wore skirts and blouses, so she didn't wince at the dresses and skirts I'd filled the closet with. She found a soft, stretchy dress that fit snuggly enough it offered a little support to her no doubt sore breasts. The royal blue color contrasted against her dark hair perfectly. It also had a low V-neck that I knew I'd be stretching out later so her tits would pop out for me to torment some more. Then I'd roll up the skirt and fuck her over the desk in the library.

I dropped a hand to my cock and started stroking myself as she finished getting dressed. A knock on the door made her start before she slowly opened it to find Henry on the other side. He quickly ran his gaze down her body and for a moment, his lips twitched as though he were struggling to hold in a smile. He'd no doubt have heard her screams during the night. I was sure he could imagine what I'd been doing to cause such a ruckus, but he was ever the professional and would never make my sweet little pet uncomfortable.

"Miss Smith, if you are ready, please follow me and we'll start the tour. First stop will be the dining room for some breakfast."

She smiled shyly at the older man. "Thank you. I am hungry so breakfast would be great."

I snickered silently, sure she'd worked up quite the appetite. I certainly had and knew what I wanted for breakfast. Following her down the hallway, I ran a finger along her spine, not stopping until it rested over her ass hole. She tensed and shuddered, but her step barely faltered as she kept walking. Excitement had me grinning. My pet was up for some games.

Moving so I hovered a breath away from her back, I reached around and palmed her tits over the dress. She gasped and reached out to place a hand on the wall as she stumbled. Henry, being the good butler he was, was instantly at her side. "Miss Smith, are you all right? Are you feeling unwell?"

She shook her head and blew out a breath. "I'm, uh, fine. Just um… saw a spider. It's gone now, so all good."

She kept her head bowed, so she didn't see Henry's smirk as he watched her nipples grow hard as I gave each a twist before I backed off again. Henry knew what us ghost monsters were like with our women. He'd seen it all before and knew what games we liked to play. I was tempted to pop her lush tits out for him as a reward but knew it was too soon. Maybe one day she'd be comfortable enough around the man to let me show her off like that.

I left her unmolested the rest of the way to the dining room. After Henry seated her and headed toward the kitchen, I moved in close again, blowing a cool breath over her neck, causing goose bumps to rise. When I was in ghost form, my touch was cool, but when I was in monster form, it was hot. It was fun to mix the two up when possible.

"Could you please stop long enough for me to eat? I'm not an exhibitionist."

I grinned, quite sure I could bring out

her inner exhibitionist, but not on our first day. I slipped my hands under her dress to give each nipple a quick twist before I pulled away just as Henry returned with Oliver, my British chef who'd trained at the finest culinary school in Paris. He was pushing a trolley laden with silver domes over plates toward us.

"Good morning, Miss Smith."

She held up a hand. "Please, call me Lisa. What's your name?"

He bowed a little. "I am Oliver, the chef here. I trust you enjoyed your meal last evening?"

She grinned broadly. "It was amazing, except I do like my steak a little more cooked."

He nodded and barely held back a wince. He liked a rare steak, as I did. I imagine Lisa best get used to not eating steak because Oliver would prefer not to cook it at all, rather than destroy it by over-cooking it.

In short order, the table before her was filled with plates of everything from Eggs Benedict to oatmeal, to pancakes. As she set about filling her plate, the men left the room, closing the door behind them. I was fairly certain they both knew what was going to happen next. Me enjoying my breakfast, as it were.

I let her get a few mouthfuls of fluffy pancakes down before I moved under the table and slid my hands up her thighs, taking the stretchy fabric of the dress with me.

"Spread your thighs, *mascota*. I want my breakfast."

"Wh-what?"

Her voice was barely more than a squeak that had me chuckling as I gripped her knees and pushed them wide, opening her pussy to me. Her curls were damp from my teasing her tits earlier and I licked my lips in anticipation. Tugging her so she was sitting on the edge of her seat, I buried my face against her pussy and began my meal.

Making my tongue thick, I thrust it deeply until I reached her cervix, where I gently tickled the surface with the very tip of my tongue. The silverware clattered to her plate a moment before she gripped the table edge. Pulling free from her core, I moved to suckle on her clit as I used two fingers to roughly finger fuck her. Reaching up with the other hand, I tugged the dress down until her tits were on full display, her tight nipples still a dark red from the previous night's activities.

Lifting my mouth for a moment, I gave her the instruction she had to know was coming.

"Torment those sweet tips for me."

Her fingers went to work, her body bucking as she teased the sensitive flesh.

"This is bizarre not being able to see you while I can feel you. And why am I just following your orders?"

I lifted from her clit but kept up the finger fucking. "Because you like it. You're my good little *mascota*."

"What—" She paused to pant. "—does that mean?"

"It's Spanish for pet, because you are my sweet, dirty, little pet, aren't you, Lisa? My good girl who'll give her master everything he wants, whenever, wherever he wants it."

With that, I pulled my fingers free and put my mouth back on her, thrusting my tongue deeply as I slipped my hand back so I could slide my slick fingers inside her ass. I couldn't wait to get back into that tight entrance again. When she orgasmed, she'd nearly strangled my cock and I'd never felt anything better.

Once I was fucking her front and back, she came in no time, gifting me with the cream I wanted for breakfast. Once I licked her clean, I pulled back and stood. Brushing her hands aside, I lapped at her nipples, loving how she shuddered at the light contact.

"Best eat quickly, *mascota*. You'll need your strength for later and Henry will return soon."

With that, I moved a step away and watched as she just sat there for a few minutes, catching her breath. She soon started eating again but didn't put her tits away or roll down her skirt, as though she'd forgotten she was exposed to the room. I wasn't about to remind her as I loved nothing more than being able to see her curves. Especially those tortured little berries that called to me.

CHAPTER
FOUR

LISA

I WAS CHEWING the last bite of pancakes when a cool breeze across my breasts reminded me that I was basically sitting here naked. Quickly, I rearranged my clothing so everything was covered, and I was certain I caught the sound of a male chuckling.

Damn ghost monster and his games.

Lifting the cup of coffee, I took a deep inhale before drinking it down.

"Hmm."

Then my dress was back down and my tits were out, my nipples being tugged and twisted by unseen hands.

"You need to not be so fucking sexy if you want a break, *mascota*."

Carefully I lowered the cup, afraid of burning myself as he continued to torture my nipples. I'd always enjoyed a little roughness, but it had been so long since I'd had any action, let alone the amount I'd had in the last twelve hours. My nipples were so sensitive, he had me ready to come with barely a touch to them now.

As soon as the cup was out of my hand, he abandoned my breasts a moment before the chair was turned and something smooth and round pressed against my mouth. Guessing it was his cock, I opened up and licked, getting a taste of salty precum that had me humming. He thrust into my mouth, stretching my lips to take his girth and going deep, just like in the car. Something wriggled between my legs under the dress, and I spread, allowing it room. It moved up and without pause entered my pussy, beginning to fuck me as his dick was my throat.

"Hands, *mascota*."

Automatically, I lifted them to my nipples, pulling and tugging as he had been doing. I gushed around whatever was fucking my pussy and he groaned and thrust deeper into my throat.

"You swallow every drop. You'll not waste a bit of my gift."

A pulse ran along the underside of his cock before he was pumping his seed straight down my throat. When he pulled free, he brushed my hands aside and took over the torment. His mouth was now getting into the action as whatever was inside me kept moving, faster now, and driving deep enough to nudge my cervix.

I'd never had a man who managed to hit it before, but I'd bumped it plenty of times with my vibrator and dildo. He'd been right when he said I liked a bite of pain. It was rare for anyone to get through the Foster Care system unscathed, and I wasn't rare. I'd been eight the first time a foster mother slapped me around. Fourteen when a foster father decided I was old enough for him to teach his son what to do with a woman. By the time I'd aged out, I was well accustomed to pain and sex. It seemed natural the two blended into some weird mix that had become my dirty secret. I'd only tried to explain it once to a boyfriend, and he was now my stalker. Lesson learned. For five years I'd had nothing but plastic or silicone between my thighs. But this monster seemed to want to give me just what I needed to reach climax without me needing to admit a damn thing. And he seemed to like doing it often.

With a hoarse shout, I came, shuddering as his mouth returned between my thighs to lap at me as I came back down. This time, he was the one to return my dress to its previous placement just as Henry came into the room. I thought I saw a sparkle in his eye, like he knew exactly what had just occurred, but if he could pretend it didn't happen, so could I.

"Are you ready for the rest of the tour, Lisa?"

I could only imagine how much fun my ghost monster was going to have with this tour, but there was no point in putting it off. Standing, I picked up my cup of coffee, which had cooled enough I could skull it down before turning back toward Henry.

"Let's do it."

With a nod and small smile, he turned, and I followed him out.

I'd seen how immense the front of the building was last night, but it was still a shock to see exactly how large it was inside. This place had wings, like some royal castle.

I paused at a wide corridor that headed off to the east. Shadows skipped across the hallway from the sunlight streaming through the windows on one side. Wanting a closer look at the artwork that hung on the walls opposite, I turned in that direction. But before I got more than a few steps, Henry was in front of me, blocking the way.

"You need to stay away from Master Cole's wing. Don't ever go down there alone, understand?"

I allowed him to guide me back in the direction we'd been heading.

"So, Cole is the owner?"

Henry dipped his chin. "He's one of several siblings who own the manor."

I tripped over my own feet, but my ghost caught me and set me upright before I could truly fall. "There's several of *them*?"

Henry's smile was tight, but humor danced in his gaze. "At the moment only three are at the manor, but you don't need to worry. They are possessive of what is theirs, and they don't share. At least not normally."

I wanted to ask what the name was of

the one who was currently following me, but how did I word that? *"Excuse me, what's the name of the ghost monster who's been fucking me senseless for the past twelve hours?"* Yeah, I'm sure that'd go over well.

With a sigh, I followed him further into the house.

"If you stay to these wider hallways and the public rooms, you'll be safe from the other siblings. They know you're claimed so won't interfere with you. But if you go into their private wings, you're basically inviting them to do as they wish with you."

I nodded, paying attention to each wing's entrance we passed so I'd remember where not to go. I had enough trouble keeping up with *my* ghost monster. I did not want or need more of them getting attached.

NOAH

It was a delight to watch Lisa's innocent reactions. For a woman so sexually adventurous, she was very naive in other aspects of life. Clearly, she didn't want to bring the attention of any of my siblings to her, which suited me just fine. Henry had spoken the truth when he'd said we didn't normally share. Only the twins liked to share their lovers. Lisa was mine alone. I would be the only one possessing her body every chance I got.

Trailing behind her and Henry, I enjoyed her every reaction to the decor and artwork throughout the large manor. I'd been around it all for so long, I barely noticed it anymore, but through Lisa's eyes, I could appreciate the effort my father had long ago put into decorating this place.

Finally, we made it to my precious library. On the very back of the manor, it rose up three stories, bookshelves covering every wall except for where there was a large stone fireplace on the lower level. The ornate timber stairs that went between each level were a work of art in themselves. The craftsman who'd originally created this space had been a master carpenter and the best in his field at the time.

"Oh, wow."

Her words were barely more than a

breath as she stood in the middle of the lower level and turned to take in all the books.

Henry moved over to where the new computer had been set up.

"If you'd come this way. Here is the computer Master ordered for your use. The software is loaded and ready for you to start entering in all the books, except those locked away on the east side of the third level. There's no time limit on getting the task completed. Master would prefer the job be done well rather than quickly."

She raised her eyebrow as though calling bullshit on that one. She already understood I wanted her here for as long as possible, so I could keep fucking her every chance I got.

Henry indicated an intercom. "If you need anything, don't hesitate to press this button and ask. Either Oliver or I will answer."

"Thank you, Henry."

With a bow, he turned and left, closing the door behind him. I stayed back, allowing Lisa time to walk around the lower level and run her fingers over the spines of random books as she moved. Finally, she went to the computer and after turning it on, sat in the comfortable chair I had placed there for her.

Once she was settled and clicking through the program, I moved in on her. Coming up behind the chair, I reached around each side to slip my hands inside her dress to palm her tits, kneading the fleshy globes as she sucked in a breath.

"Starting to think you're fixated."

I ran my tongue up her neck as I gave each nipple a rough twist.

"Of course, I am. Your tits are magnificent. I could play with them all day, every day."

She chuckled then groaned when I tweaked her nipples again. "I think even I would get too sore after a whole day of constant nipple play."

"Hmm, we'll have to test that out at some point."

She shook her head as she started to rub her thighs together.

"Stand up and remove your dress. I want you naked whenever we're alone."

She stood but hesitated as she gripped the bottom hem of her dress. "I want to see you too. It's messing with my head that I can feel but not see you."

By the time she had her dress up over her head, I was standing in front of her, in all my naked monster glory. This was the first time she was seeing me clearly, the high skylights filling the entire library with sunlight enough for her to see every inch of me. Her gaze traveled from the tips of my horns, over my face then down to the pads of my pecs. In the dull light last night, she wouldn't have been able to see the fine black lines that were the veins that ran close to my skin's surface. It was how my body maintained its heat. My blood ran hotter than a human's and running so close to the surface of my flesh, it meant I radiated heat. The faster my blood pumped, the hotter I got.

Her fingers twitched and I reached for her hand, pulling her forward until I could place her palm against my pec.

"I wondered if I'd imagined it last night, but you really do run hotter than normal, don't you?"

I nodded as a shudder ran through me as she stroked my chest. "I was once as human as you. It was only after I died in a fire that destroyed our stable that I discovered my father had employed a witch to curse us. Well, he believed it was a blessing, to ensure none of his children would die young as his wife, my mother, had. So here we all are, alive long after we should have passed from old age."

"You're all ghost monsters?"

She now had both palms on me, stroking every dip and curve of my arms, chest and torso, learning me as I had her in the car yesterday.

"Of a sort. We're all unique. Tied to different elements due to the manner in which we died. But we all have a ghost form and a monster form."

I nodded as her lids hooded and her palms dropped down over my hips before she drew them in and wrapped both palms around my hard dick. I growled in pleasure as she attempted to stroke me with her small hands.

While she was tall for a human female, at maybe five feet eight, she was still a lot shorter than my seven feet two. But not so short that she didn't fit against me perfectly, which she proved when she released my cock to move in close. Her breasts came up against my torso, while my rock-hard cock throbbed against the softness of her stomach.

CHAPTER
FIVE

LISA

"GOOD THING I like the heat then, huh?"

And that was the truth. If it was cold outside, I was inside with the heater cranked up. Now I had my very own personal heater. I was naked in an open room yet was toasty warm this close to my ghost monster.

I looked up at his face. "You've never told me your name. What is it?"

I couldn't keep calling him ghost monster.

He grinned down, his dark eyes sparkling with humor.

"Noah Gallichan at your service, ma'am."

The falsely thick southern drawl had me

chuckling until he groaned and tightened his grip on me.

"It's been too long since I've been inside you, and I didn't get enough at breakfast."

Before I could respond, he lifted me off the floor. Then, after flashing me a wicked smirk, he spun me around so my face was in front of his gargantuan, erect cock while his face had to be lined up with my pussy. This position wasn't going to be fun for long. Blood was already rushing to my head.

He banded an arm around my waist, holding me against him as he covered my pussy with his mouth and that deviously talented tongue of his went deep inside me, instantly lighting me up.

Blowing out a breath, I reached to grip his dick, bringing the head to my mouth where I started to lap at him while I trailed my other hand underneath until I had his large balls in my palm. Well, I could only fit one in my palm at a time so I gently rolled each one in turn as I widened my lips and took as much of his length into my mouth as I could at this angle.

When something slithered around my neck, I jerked off his cock. Looking down, I saw what must have been his tail wind around from behind him toward my neck. It tightened slightly — not enough to affect my breathing — then pulled me back toward his body, clearly wanting me to get back to sucking his dick. When I took his length back in as deeply as I could, the tip of his tail moved from around my neck to my breasts. A groan vibrated through me when the tip started slapping at my tender nipples. Clearly liking my reaction, he did it again and again, thrusting his hips forward each time I groaned.

I struggled to stay focused as he continued to eat me out with his tongue and lips, then he had a finger slipping into my ass and my whole body convulsed as I came. I screamed and he slipped his cock further down my throat where the pulsing warned me, he was about to come too. The hot jets came fast, and it was a struggle to swallow while upside down but I somehow managed, knowing he wouldn't want me to waste any.

As my body came back online, I could feel he was still lapping at my pussy, and he now had three fingers fucking my ass. The sensations were too much and the blood rushing to my head wasn't helping things.

"Noah, enough. I need to be the right way up!"

With a grunt, he manhandled me until I was the right way up, my legs over his shoulders so his mouth was still over my pussy. I gripped his horns to steady myself as he continued eating me out and fucking my ass with his thick fingers. Sweat slicked my skin and when my hand slipped over his horn, his whole body shivered so I moved my other hand over the other horn, grinning when he shivered again.

Since his horns were sensitive, as he continued to torment my pussy and ass, I set about stroking and petting his horns, letting my fingers bounce over the ridges before I gripped them like I would his dick, and twisting my hands.

With a growl, he tore his mouth from my core and lowered me down his body. I'd barely taken a breath when he impaled my pussy with his cock, thrusting up in one move until he bottomed out.

"Naughty little *mascota*. Teasing your master's horns."

He moved across the room, each step pushing his cock harder against my cervix and sending me closer to coming. Then he was laying me back over a counter that put my body at the perfect height for him to fuck me. He put my feet up over his shoulders and pulled my butt back to the edge of the countertop then he started pounding into me, hard and fast.

"So soft and wet for me. You like this, *mascota*? You like when your monster owns you?"

"Uh huh." Was all I could muster.

With another growl, he pulled from my pussy and tilted my hips up a moment before he lined his huge cock up with my ass and pushed in until he was buried to the hilt.

"Hmm, love how your ass takes all of me. Such a good little *mascota.*"

I really shouldn't like him calling me his pet as much as I did, but honestly, he had me in a constant state of arousal to the point I really don't give a fuck about anything other than getting his dick inside me again.

My ex had accused me of being a nymphomaniac for how much I liked sex. It was one of the reasons he'd given for why he'd pimped me out. Tried to tell me it was his way of taking care of my needs. Like he wasn't focused on all the money he was making off me.

No matter what he did though, even before he turned into an abusive asshole, he'd never managed to satisfy me. Not like Noah already had. Who knew I'd just needed a rough, possessive supernatural monster who never seemed to go soft to fully satisfy my needs?

Reaching around my legs, he grabbed my breasts and used them to pull me back into him as he thrust into me, then he grabbed my nipples, twisting and squeezing until I was writhing against the bench and his cock. When his tail entered my pussy, growing thicker until it was fucking me as though it was another cock, I whimpered and shattered into orgasm.

NOAH

Had to say, I was more than a little proud I'd managed to knock out my little pet with pleasure. I sat in the large chair in front of the fireplace, her body draped over me, her back to my front. Her legs were over mine and spread wide so my tail could continue to stroke her inner walls, keeping her pleasure going, sending more shudders through her body. My hands were on her tits, stroking her gently until her nipples elongated, then pinching and twisting them to heighten her arousal.

She really was perfect and for the first time in my long life, I wondered about whether I should mate this one. It would mean being able to have children, a family, and also would mean her life would be tied to mine so she'd live as long as I did.

Sensing Cole coming near, I turned to where I knew his ghost form stood, taking in the beauty writhing over me.

"She is pretty, brother."

With a wicked grin, I responded telepathically, *"She's a dirty little nymphomaniac."*

"Never would have guessed she was hiding that behind her sweet words and prissy clothes."

He'd joined me once or twice when I'd gone to check on her. I shook my head his way. *"You didn't look closely then. You need to learn how to notice the little things that give a woman away. The way they walk with that extra sway, the way her underwear was all lace and skimpy. Her toy collection. The way she clearly preferred those toys to trying to find a man. Human men can't keep up with our women, their needs are too great."*

Cole's deep chuckle was the only response there was time for before Lisa began to wake, and his presence left the room. I continued to stroke her tits but stopped torturing her nipples. By this point, they'd be so tender, even the gentle strokes I was delivering would have her arousal shooting skyward.

She rolled her head, pressing her face in against my throat as she undulated and had another small orgasm, dousing my tail in her cream. Slipping my tail out, I widened the tip and slapped the pad of her pussy just over her clit a few times, grinning at the moan and full body jerk it earned me.

"You back with me, *mascota*?"

"Hmm."

She rolled onto her side, curling up against my chest to snuggle down and go to sleep.

"I thought you'd be more excited over all the books, to be honest," I mused aloud.

"I was before you wore me out. Now I need a nap," she mumbled as she spoke against my chest, her breath tickling me.

I started running my fingers through her hair before stroking down her back. My tail came up to start teasing where her thighs were pressed together before slipping through her slit to rub over her entrance and clit. I kept the strokes light and slow, knowing she most likely did need to rest but unable to resist touching her when she was so close.

"You're insatiable."

She muttered the words like she was complaining but she shifted to her front, moving her legs to straddle my hips so she could sit up and impale herself onto my cock. Gripping her hips, I took control of her movements, making sure she took me deeply enough to give her all she needed. Most women hated having their cervix tapped but Lisa clearly loved it. Which suited me because there was no greater feeling than having the head of my dick hit that soft flesh deep inside a woman.

"Hands on your tits, *mascota.*"

She reached up to cup herself, kneading her lush tits before she moved to the nipples. As she gave them each a twist, I slid my tail up between her ass cheeks, teasing the entrance there with the tip. She shuddered and moaned as I slipped inside her ass before widening the flesh to fill her completely. Reaching up, I gripped her jaw, forcing it open until I could slide my thumb in.

"Suck."

Just like in the car, she got to work on my thumb, as she rode my cock, and I fucked her ass with my tail.

Fuck, I was never going to get tired of fucking her. Definitely needed to look into what mating entailed. Whenever it had come up before I'd ignored it, not wanting anything to do with it. But watching her ride me like this, I couldn't help but imagine how she'd look with a belly rounded with our child. First, I needed to work out if the child would be human or monster before I went there with her.

"You look so pretty with your holes full, you make me wish I had three cocks."

With my free hand, I started toying with her clit until her eyes teared up and her body shook with the start of her orgasm. Pulling my thumb free from her mouth, I sat up straighter, latching my mouth onto her right tit and biting down until I pierced her skin and got a taste of her sweet blood while I pulled her down as far as I could onto my erection. Screaming my name, she gripped my horns while she came all over me. Her cream dripped down my cock and over my balls as I lapped at her wound, sealing it closed before I lifted her off my dick and slid my tail from her ass.

Panting, she slumped against me.

"I'm never going to even get started on the books if you keep this up."

I chuckled and stood with her in my arms. "You were the one who started that round, *mascota*."

As I passed through the door, she tensed. "Noah, I'm naked!"

"Trust me, I know. We're not going far. Relax."

Little did she know, Cole had already seen her in all her glory, and no doubt my other siblings would be seeing all of her before long, considering I couldn't help but fuck her every chance I got.

Ducking into the bathroom next to the library, I flipped on the shower and took her in with me to clean her up.

CHAPTER
SIX

LISA

After a very long shower that included another orgasm for me, I was finally back in the library. I'd put the dress back on, despite Noah's complaints. I needed some sort of barrier against him so I could at least look at this computer system. I had a job to do here, other than fucking my monster. I was a librarian for a reason. I loved books and all the knowledge they contained. They'd saved my sanity more times than I could count during my childhood. I couldn't wait to dive into finding what gems were hidden in this room.

With a deep inhale of the delightful aroma of old books, I settled at the desk and turned my focus to working out how to use the software that had already been loaded onto the machine. It wasn't anything I'd used before but that didn't matter. It appeared to be similar to the last system I used. Standing from the desk, I glanced around the huge space. Where to begin?

I startled when cool hands wrapped around my hips. I shouldn't have been surprised that Noah had returned to his ghost form to spy on me. Cool breath bathed my ear as he turned me to the left.

"Start there, *mascota*. I'll be back later to try out what you learn."

Then his touch was gone, and a shudder ran through me as my arousal coiled within me with nowhere to go. Surely, after all the sex I'd had in the last day, my body would be sated. Apparently not. The mere thought of Noah had my body heating and softening in welcome, wanting his cock again.

With a sigh and shake of my head, I made my way over to the shelves where he'd indicated I should start. Pulling the book from the end of the top shelf, I read the title and laughed. Naturally, he had a collection based on the original Kama Sutra. Taking an armful of books, I returned to the desk and entered the details into the system before I had a quick flick through the pages. Several of the positions Noah had already bent me into jumped out at me and I grinned as a few others caught my attention.

Tonight was going to be fun.

Humming, I happily sank into the work, logging in books and flipping through the pages, keeping aside several I wanted to take a closer look at. Some of the books were first editions and needed to be handled carefully, while others were near new. Clearly, he'd gotten me to start in the erotic part of the library, and I found everything from the Kama Sutra stuff through to various kink and BDSM lifestyle guides.

Completely lost in my own head, a knock on the frame of the open door had me jumping. I looked up to see Henry standing there carrying a covered tray.

"Excuse me, Lisa, but you haven't called down for food yet and it's getting late, so I've brought you a small something to keep you going until you require your evening meal."

He came and set it down on the desk with such smooth efficiency before he turned and left me alone again that I never found my voice to thank the man. Lifting the lid, I sighed at the aroma that hit me. I wasn't sure what it was called, but the little pastry cups were filled with something cream-based that smelled divine and I quickly ate all five of them. Once I finished, I moved the tray over to another table before returning to work. I figured I might as well keep going until Noah came to find me. I knew once he did, I wouldn't be getting any more work done.

As I went to sit back into my chair, my dress was hitched up and before I knew what was going on, it was over my head and landing in a pile on the floor as I was pulled down to sit on my monster's lap. His thick erection rubbed over my pussy as I came to rest against him.

"You unfairly use your ghost form."

His hands, now in monster form, went straight to my breasts, where he started to stroke my flesh until my nipples elongated, before he switched to pinching and twisting them. It was more than I could take and stay sane. Reaching down, I gripped his dick in my hand before I lifted up, tilting my hips until the head of his cock was against my entrance. As soon as it was lined up, I lowered myself down over his length, taking him deep inside.

"I'll use any means I can in order to get inside you, *mascota*. Lean forward and grip the edge of the desk."

I did as he instructed and he stood, shoving the chair away and then began to pound into me. My breasts swung with each thrust, the weight of them tugging uncomfortably at my chest. The moment I whimpered, he shifted his hands to cup each of my mounds in his large palms, using his grip on them to hold me still while he fucked me hard and fast.

With a growl, he pulled free and spun me around before he lifted me up and pulled me back onto his cock. The way he so easily held my weight up off the ground made my heart trip over a beat. He behaved like I was a featherweight, when I knew, even with what I'd recently lost, I was anything but. I grabbed onto his biceps as he pulled me up and down his erection, fucking me as though I was a toy. And for some fucked-up reason, that did it for me because it was only minutes later that I shattered apart for him, clenching down on his dick as I came. The feel of his hot seed filling me prolonged the pleasure until a second, smaller climax rippled through me.

"You're done working for today."

With that, he tossed me over his shoulder and headed for the door.

"Noah! I'm naked!"

A firm swat to my ass was his only response before he strode out the library and into the main part of the manor with me draped over his shoulder, both of us naked as the day we were born, and me with his cum leaking out of my pussy and down onto his shoulder.

I smacked at his back. "At least let me put my dress back on."

He swatted my butt again, in the same spot. The sting sent a tingle up my spine I didn't want to admit to enjoying. "The more noise you make, the more likely someone will come to see what's going on. Stay silent and no one will see what belongs to me."

Relaxing against his shoulder, I gave in and allowed him to carry me off like some sort of Neanderthal. I guess I should be grateful he didn't first club me over the head or drag me off by my hair.

NOAH

The days blurred into weeks, then months as I continued to fuck my little pet senseless every chance I got. She insisted on doing at least a few hours of work in the library each day. I always followed and watched over her. She was passionate about her work, and seeing how excited she got over many of the books in my collection had my dick constantly hard. Some days I couldn't resist and would interrupt her several times so I could get inside of her. She never complained. Well, she never complained once I had my cock or tongue inside her, at least.

Lisa was my perfect match. While she worked on cataloging the lower and mid levels, I spent time on the upper level, in the locked section where I had father's diaries stored. I'd been researching everything about mating and what it entailed, not that there was much. Father hadn't given a fuck about us having kids. Guess he figured with us being immortal, it wouldn't matter. I was currently going back over the diary he'd written around the time he'd had the curse put on us all, looking for anything I might have missed when I'd read it previously.

I shook my head as a familiar rage settled over me at my father and all the pain he'd unwittingly brought upon his children, all in the name of avoiding having to experience the loss of any more of his kin himself.

Why couldn't he have grieved like a normal man?

Closing my eyes, I tried to remember my mother. She'd died in the summer of 1742 in a boating accident, I'd been barely a teenager at the time. My youngest sibling, still a babe. This year was my two-hundred-fifty-fifth year since my own death and rebirth in this form. Plenty of time for my human memories to fade to near nothing.

On waking from the fire that killed me and discovering what Father had done, rage engulfed me completely and I'd become a mindless beast, burning my way through the countryside for years before my temper cooled enough I could think clearly. I winced as I contemplated how many legends and ghost stories I was responsible for.

By the time the last of my siblings had died and come back in their monster form, I'd settled and returned to help each of them with the transition. It was the twins who'd found the witch responsible. They'd hoped to undo the curse, but it was impossible, Father had been careful with how he had the witch cast her magic. That hadn't stopped the witch's coven-sister feeling sorry for the twins and going after our father, killing him using her magic so he'd never be able to return to the mortal realm in any form.

Now that I thought about it, I remembered the witch had told the twins about the mating side of things, saying that was a blessing within our curse.

I scoffed. Blessing, my ass. But I needed to speak with the twins. Thankfully, they were currently here at the manor so I could handle this now. After the months it had taken to read all the diaries and not discovering the information I wanted, I was quickly getting frustrated.

Lisa was unlike any lover I'd ever taken before. She was unique in this world, and I didn't want to ever live without her. I knew if something happened to her, I wouldn't recover from the loss. That thought gave me pause. Was that how Father had felt after losing Mother?

I shook my head. No. I would not feel sorry for the man who'd cursed all his children to be monsters.

Returning the diary to its shelf, I re-locked the door before floating over to the other side of the top level where I found my sweet pet stretching to reach a book on a high shelf. She was wearing a shirt and skirt, the top lifting to bare a strip of tempting flesh as she tried to do without the ladder she should be using. Sneaking up behind her, I took my monster form a moment before I touched her warm skin. She shrieked in surprise, tensing for a moment before relaxing as I ran my palms up to her tits. She'd long ago succumbed to my demand she not wear any underwear around the house. She still grumbled on occasion that she was too big to not wear a bra, but I didn't give a fuck. I wanted easy access twenty-four/seven. She benefited from the arrangement as much as I did.

Giving each nipple a hard twist, I inhaled deeply as her arousal filled the air around us.

Lowering my face, I blew hot air over her neck before speaking, "Why didn't you use the ladder, *mascota*?"

"I thought I could reach."

Reaching her right hand up, she rubbed my horn as though she had my cock in her palm. A full body shudder ran through me at the contact. She was relentless now she knew how I reacted to having my horns played with. As she continued to twist her palm around my horn, I tore her shirt from her body, baring her lush tits to my view as I continued to pinch, tug and twist her hard little nubs. Since moving into Gallichan Manor and eating more, her curves had filled out and I couldn't be happier.

Releasing her tits, I made fast work of tearing her skirt until it lay in pieces around us. With a gasp, she released my horn and looked around.

"Noah! I liked that skirt. And that top. What's gotten into you?"

"Need you."

I'd buy her replacements later. Picking her up, I quickly moved down the stairs to the table in the center of the lower level. Like a doll, she let me maneuver her until she was in a yoga child's pose on the edge of the timber, her ass and pussy on display for me. The arch of her spine as she reached her hands forward along the glossy table had me gripping my cock and giving it a few rough tugs. My little pet was so perfect.

Her pussy glistened in the sunlight streaming through the skylights, but she wasn't wet enough yet. With a wicked grin that probably would have scared her if she could see me, I started to spank her perfect, lush ass with the flat of my hand. She yelped on the first few strikes, like she always did, then with a sigh, she relaxed into it. I kept going until her ass was a rich red, matching my own skin. Lowered down, I bit the warmed skin hard enough to draw blood, that I sucked down a mouthful of before I lapped at the small wound, sealing it.

Running my hand under her pussy, I got a palm full of cream.

"You do love a good spanking."

"Not as much as I love a good fuck."

I chuckled. She was getting bolder with her talk. Long gone was the sweet lady who avoided cussing when she'd first arrived. She'd explained that was a persona she'd taken on when she started working in libraries. This crass, sexy siren was the true her.

With our height difference, she was at the perfect level for me to take her. Without any warning, I slammed in deep, filling her pussy until I bottomed out on one stroke. I held still to enjoy the way she rippled around me. Then when I started to move, taking her hard and rough, just the way we both liked it, she began to whimper and claw at the tabletop, trying to find something to grip.

Running my hand up her spine, I kept going until I could wrap my palm around the back of her neck, holding her in place as I wound my tail around to tease her ass hole while I continued to fuck her pussy.

She hummed as the tip of my tail

slipped inside to stroke the inner walls of her back entrance.

"More."

Her voice was more of a groan rather than words, but I heard her, and I always gave my little pet what she needed. Shifting my grip around to the front of her neck, I lifted her up against me, her knees slipping wide on the glossy tabletop as I brought her back up against my front while I never paused in fucking both her holes. With just enough pressure on her throat for her to know I was in total control of our encounter, I leaned down to nip at the edge of her ear.

"Hands on your tits, *mascota*."

Once she was working over her nipples roughly, I slipped my other hand down until I could pinch at her clit in time with my deep thrusts inside her. It only took a few strokes like this before she threw her head back against my shoulder and screamed out my name as she shattered for me. I kept at her, not slowing until a tingle shot down my spine, landing in my balls a moment before I came, filling her womb with my cum.

CHAPTER
SEVEN

LISA

SOMETHING HAD GOTTEN into my monster. I had no clue what, but it wasn't like him to tear my clothes off me like he had earlier. Normally, he'd either strip me or tell me to strip. I never denied him. Why would I when I was going to get what I wanted if I did what he told me? But now I was left with no clothes to wear later when I'd need to return to our wing on the opposite side of the house.

Bastard had ghosted on me again after he fucked me senseless on the library table. Told me to finish my workday and that he'd be back to lead me back to our room like I really was a pet that he needed to leash and collar or something. I'd learned that it was near impossible to resist an order delivered while he was in ghost form. I'd only managed it once, and that was when he tried to order me to go without underwear when I had to go into town to see a doctor for a check-up and my birth control shot. I had no idea if he could actually impregnate me, but considering he filled my womb with cum several times a day, I figured staying on birth control was a good idea. For now.

I'd gotten a wicked headache that nearly had me canceling the damn appointment when I'd resisted his order, but dammit, I was not going to see a doctor without a bra or panties!

Considering I had nothing else to do but my job here in the library if he was gone, I didn't even try to object to this particular order. Although, I did make a quick trip out to the bathroom to clean up before returning to my desk where I found the book I'd been trying to reach earlier sitting next to my keyboard.

That made me smile. My monster did have a sweet side. My freshly spanked ass smarted when I lowered into the seat, but the ache wasn't so distracting I couldn't work. Getting lost in these books—the old and the new—was a true joy. Noah had collected research tomes on all sorts of subjects, not just sex. Each day I learned something new and fascinating, and I was dreading the day I'd finish with cataloging it all.

That thought had me sitting back in my seat. What was I going to do when this was done? The initial letter only invited me to stay for as long as it took to complete the job. Had that changed now I was Noah's *mascota*, his pet?

Chewing my thumb nail, I pondered that thought. It wasn't like I'd left anything behind to come here, and I really didn't want to leave. Lifting my gaze to the third level, I took in how few rows remained. The job was nearly done. Maybe I should have worked slower, dragged it out so I could stay longer. But would prolonging my departure just make the heartache worse? Would leaving sooner be better?

My vision blurred and I dashed the tears away before they could fall. The last thing I needed was for Noah to see me crying like a baby over something that was a condition from the start. He might kick me to the curb earlier.

"There you are, my little slut."

The voice was like ice down my spine, and I jerked up out of the seat to face the threat before I knew what I was doing.

Christopher's face pulled into an ugly sneer as he stood just inside the doorway.

"Look at you. Naked and ready to go. Fuck, it smells like an orgy in here and I can see the cum on you. You been giving away what isn't yours to sell, babe?"

His to sell? I shook my head as fear and anger mixed together in my belly, causing me to cramp as nausea rose.

"Christopher, I haven't been yours for a long damn time. And I was never yours to sell. That's why I left. What are you even doing here?" *How the hell did you find me this time?*

He prowled toward me slowly as though he knew I had nowhere to go, and he had all the time in the world.

"I'm here to collect what's mine, of course. Nice try hiding out in this old place, but I'll always find you, babe. You're mine.

Always will be. And whoever has been fucking you will pay for the privilege."

My breath stuttered at the reminder I wasn't alone this time. I had a monster to help me. Noah would never allow this bastard to take me. Christopher had no idea the hell that would be unleashed. I wasn't sure where Noah had gone, but clearly it wasn't anywhere nearby, or he'd already be here. I needed to get out of this room and start calling out to him.

My need to get away from Christopher had me ignoring the fact I was buck-ass naked. Christopher had seen it all before, and thanks to Noah carrying me around the mansion naked over his shoulder regularly, I was certain everyone else in the place had seen all of me too.

I stepped to the side as he got closer, skirting around the big table Noah had fucked me on earlier. My heart ached when my gaze caught on the marks we'd left on the shiny surface as I moved around the opposite side to Christopher.

"Looks like you gave the table a workout. Maybe I'll give you a go up there myself. What do you say? Or you want me to bring a few of my buddies over first, give you a train like you love."

Anger built higher as his words had me remembering the torture he'd heaped on me.

"I fucking hated everything you and your sleazy friends did to me, you bastard."

He threw his head back to laugh like he'd already won. I made the most of him being distracted and started to dash for the door. Before I made it more than three steps, he was on me, tackling my body with his and taking us both down to the ground. My glasses went flying but I didn't have time to worry about them.

"Fuck, you're covered in cum, little slut. Normally I don't like sloppy seconds, but you're not giving me a choice. Need to fuck some sense into you. Remind you who you belong to. Because you will be coming home with me today."

Refusing to give in, I wriggled and bucked against his hold. No way would I leave the manor with him. I'd rather die here than be his captive. The sound of his zipper opening had a shiver running down my spine. Him preparing to rape me had panic rising up, which gave me the burst of strength I needed. Focusing my gaze, I planned my attack. Rather than mindless thrashing, I aimed my knee for his now exposed cock and balls. He caught onto my intention and moved, but not fast enough to avoid the blow entirely. The strike was hard enough he rolled away with a curse, and I was on my feet in seconds and out the door, skidding on the polished floor as I sprinted up the hallway.

"Noah! Cole! Henry! Oliver! Anyone! Help me!"

I screamed out the names of everyone I hoped might be in the house. I wished I knew the names of all Noah's siblings. Henry had said three were home, but I only knew Cole's name. Still, surely if they heard me screaming, they'd come, even if they didn't hear their name?

Noah's wing was all the way across the house, but Cole's was just up ahead. I knew I needed to get off this main hallway before Christopher pulled himself together.

"Noah!" I called out before turning down the main hallway of Cole's domain and sprinting again.

"Bitch!"

A shiver ran down my spine at how close Christopher's voice sounded. Feeling exposed in the main hall, I turned into the next room I reached, shoving the door open and rushing inside, barely skidding to a stop before I went face first into a pond. Well, it was big enough to be a pool, but it had lily pads and plants around the edges. Maybe I could submerge myself and hide from Christopher. I could hold my breath for a little while. If I got under one of the larger lily pads, I could sneak breaths without him seeing if he came in. Maybe.

"You shouldn't be here, little one. Especially disrobed as you are."

The voice held the same accent as Noah's, but it didn't affect me like his did.

"Cole?"

Ripples in the water were my only warning before a blue, horned face rose above the surface. He stopped when his torso was fully out of the water, and I thought I saw several tentacles move below the surface. Before I could look closer, he moved forward in rush, causing me to jerk and slip on the polished marble. With a curse, I was falling toward the water before I could stop my descent.

Cool arms wrapped around me, "Take a deep breath."

Suspecting what he was about to do, I did as instructed and just as the door to the hall began to open, the monster holding me smoothly slipped under the surface with me in his embrace. He quickly glided to the rear of the pool, between the largest of the lily pads and I saw Christopher's blurry figure move around the perimeter of the room.

NOAH

Lisa's scream echoed through the mansion, and I jumped to my feet from where I'd been sitting, talking to the twins.

"Is this some game your woman is playing with you?"

I shook my head at my brother. "No, she's in distress."

And I'd left her naked. Fuck. Taking ghost form, I flew through the halls to the library, but arrived to find it empty. The marks on the floor near the door and the fact her glasses lay abandoned on the tile indicated there'd been a struggle of some sort. I followed the footprints my pet's bare feet had made on the polished floor. The twins were behind me, ready to help if needed, and I appreciated the back-up, although I doubted I'd need it. Any bastard stupid enough to hurt what was mine would get torn limb from limb.

Frowning, I continued to follow my pet into Cole's wing. What was she thinking? Going into a monster's lair uninvited was courting trouble on an epic level. While Cole had been a complete gentleman in his human life, he was now a monster like the rest of us. My heart nearly ceased beating when I saw the door to the room that housed his pond swing shut. She'd gone into water with him? Fuck. Depending on what Cole decided to do, Lisa had either chosen the best or worst place to hide, assuming that was what she was attempting to do.

"Does she know Cole?"

I shook my head before answering the twins, *"Not that I know of. I shall soon find out."*

"I know you're in here, little slut. You left

footprints any fool could follow, so stop hiding and come out."

The male voice was pissed off, but it was no one I knew. Ghosting through the door, I saw a bulky human male storming around the outside of the room, looking behind every leaf and plant. A ripple at the rear of the pond caught my gaze and relief poured through me as Cole carefully lifted Lisa's nose and mouth above the surface near a lily pad for a moment before lowering back down.

Relief briefly flared through me that Cole had decided to protect her, not attempt to claim her. With Lisa safe in my brother's arms, I was free to deal with the fucker who was hunting my mate. Yeah, I may not have claimed her yet, but I would. Just as soon as I dealt with this human piece of shit. Moving to stand in front of the only exit, I shimmered into my monster form and waited for the bastard to notice me.

"You're gonna pay for this, bitch. You think what I did before was torture? Just wait till I get you back home this time. You won't be able to put your legs together ever again once I get done."

Fury flowed through me, heating my blood enough that the leaves near me dried out and turned black. I roared out my challenge, taking a small amount of joy in the way the human male stilled before he turned to face me wide-eyed as he urinated himself.

Curling my lip in disgust, I stormed over to where he stood, ready to end the fucker who had clearly terrorized Lisa in the past.

"You come into my home and try to take my woman? Threaten her with harm in front of me?"

He shook his head before he snapped out of his shock and turned to run away. Fool thought he could beat me back to the door and escape. A shimmer in the air revealed the twins in their full monster glory in front of the door, blocking the only exit. With a high-pitched squeal that didn't fit his size, the man stopped and turned so he could switch his gaze between the twins and me, clearly unsure who was the bigger threat.

"What the fuck are you?"

Hearing our voices, Cole must have guessed he no longer needed to keep Lisa hidden from view. He rose from the pond, Lisa wrapped in his arms, cradled against his muscular chest as she gasped in a few deep breaths. She wiped her palm over her face, pushing the water away before glaring over at the man.

"Who are they? They're my family. Unlike you, they protect those they care for, not abuse them. The big, red one is the one who's been fucking me. You still going to make him pay for that? I dare you to try, Christopher."

My heart swelled at her calling us her family. She'd never seen the twins or Cole before today, but she instinctively knew where to lay her trust. I was grateful Cole hadn't seen her as a sexual partner like I did. Naked as she was, things could have easily gone down a lot darker path when she'd stormed into my brother's personal space.

Rage mottled Christopher's face red but he didn't dare to attack. Guess he knew he was outnumbered and outmuscled. No way could he win against a monster, let alone an enraged one who had a woman to protect. Who also had three brothers to back him up.

"You bitch. What did you do? Whore yourself out to fucking monsters for their protection?" He ran his gaze over the twins and me, taking in our naked forms including our dicks, that even flaccid, were bigger than human males were. "You really are a fucking slut. Not sure why you took such issue with what I had you do." At my growl, he stopped talking.

"You will die for what you've done. Run, if you wish. I do enjoy a chase, and Cole won't like your blood in his pond if I kill you here."

The twins had ghosted and opened the door in invitation. Christopher did a double take when he glanced and saw the way was clear. He took off, sprinting out into the hallway. Before I followed, I turned to Cole. "Keep her safe for me. I'll return for her shortly."

He gave me a nod then I was striding through the door. With my height, I barely needed to jog in order to catch up with the little fucker aiming for the front doors of the manor. Henry came rushing through the door from the servant's quarters. "Master Noah, do you need my assistance?"

I shook my head as I passed. "Not yet, but depending on where I catch this bastard, you may be needed on clean-up later."

"Of course. I'll wait on your orders."

Henry was the perfect butler. Nothing ruffled his feathers, which was a positive, all things considered.

CHAPTER
EIGHT

LISA

CLINGING TO COLE as I took some deep breaths into my burning lungs, my gaze followed Noah as he stalked out after Christopher.

"Cole, please let me go. I need—"

"You need to what? Go help? Trust me, little sister, Noah can handle that piece of shit all on his own."

I struggled against his hold, trying to break free to leave the pond until with a sigh, he began to move toward the steps leading out of the water.

"If you insist on going, I need to come with you. I'll be in my ghost form but don't think I can't still stop you from doing anything stupid, like interfering with what Noah is doing. You understand the bloodshed you're going to walk in on?"

Striding up the steps, I tried to shake off water from my legs and arms as I wrung out my hair the best I could. Thankfully, my eyesight wasn't terrible. My glasses had gotten lost in the fight in the library, so the world was a touch blurry but not so much that I couldn't make out the big, blue monster sliding up the steps on tentacles. Yep, he seriously had a heap of tentacles instead of two legs. My mind wandered for a moment as I thought about what Noah could do with his tail if he had that many of them…

A low growl brought me out of my daydream. "Lisa, stop it. You are Noah's woman, and he doesn't share what's his. But I only have so much self-restraint."

I shook my head to clear it. "Sorry, okay. So… going to find Noah now."

I headed to the door and as I passed through it, a towel was draped over my shoulders. With a smile, I grabbed the fabric and wrapped it around my body, covering everything important as I headed to the front door that had been left open.

Before I could make it, Henry stood in my way.

"Lisa, you don't want to go out there."

I looked up at his serious gray eyes. "I need to see what's going on."

He shook his head. "You really don't. You know what's going to happen. Noah is going to win and then he'll be back for you. If I allow you out there to see him in full monster mode, he'll never forgive me when you reject him."

I stamped my foot in frustration. What was with these men? Did they think I hadn't already noticed his horns and tail? I got Noah was a monster.

"What if I don't? What if the fact he'd go to such lengths to keep me safe makes me love him even more?"

He sighed then shook his head in a way that gave me hope I'd won this argument. "Women. So very stubborn. Try not to get us all killed, yeah?"

I patted his shoulder as I moved past and out the door into the late afternoon sunlight. I could hear male voices coming from the right side of the manor but not what was being said, then an agonized scream filled the air, and I took off running toward the sound.

Skidding to a stop when I caught sight of them both, I stayed still as I took it in. The man who'd made my life hell then stalked me for years was now crawling through the dirt, crying as he tried to escape. There were four deep gashes across his right thigh that were pouring blood over the ground as he moved, trying to get away from Noah. My monster had grown at least another foot in height, and now sported long, black claws instead of nails and his teeth were now pointed and bared as though he were part wolf. His sole focus was on taking down my stalker.

"What did you say you were going to do to my woman?" His voice held a lisp now, as though he struggled to talk around all those sharp, pointy teeth.

"N-nothing! It was all talk. I'd never really hurt her. She's mine, she knows she's mine. She just needs a little reminding. That's all."

His words had my own fury building

until I *had* to do something. Looking around until I found a rock the right size, I picked it up then threw it with all my might toward the man who'd been the bane of my existence for so long now. It hit him in the shoulder and had him and Noah jerking to look my way in stunned silence.

Glaring straight into Christopher's face, I growled out my words, "How dare you, you piece of shit! Never hurt me? You pimped me out to your buddies, told them to be as rough as they wanted! They tore me up so badly that last time I had to be sewn up. It was the staff at the hospital that helped me get away from you. Even they were sure you'd kill me next time."

My words dried up at the roar that filled the night. A blast of heat knocked me down onto my butt as I looked up at Noah in shock. Had he gotten even bigger? Between one blink and the next, he was on Christopher and screams echoed around me as Noah went into a frenzy, tearing the man beneath him to ribbons. Covered in his blood, he finally stopped and lifting his head to the sky, let loose a roar that was so mournful, my eyes teared.

I'd forced him to perpetrate such violence. He'd always been so gentle with me. Sure, the sex was rough, but he'd never once actually hurt me. Now I'd forced him to kill a man. Henry had worried I wouldn't be able to forgive Noah, but my real concern was the other way around. Would Noah be able to forgive me for this?

Tears tracked down my cheeks as I buried my face in my palms and cried for what I'd just lost. Noah would surely send me away now. I'd be alone again. My breath caught in my lungs when I was lifted up off the ground.

"Lisa, *mi alma*, what's wrong? I didn't hurt you, did I?"

Clinging to him, I shook my head, not caring that we were now both covered in blood. My arms wrapped around his neck as he ran his palms over every inch of me, checking for injury. The towel I'd been wrapped in was gone but I didn't care, I need to feel him, the warmth of his skin against mine.

"Don't send me away. I'm sorry."

He stilled. Even his chest stopped moving at my words and I risked opening an eye to look up at him. He was staring at me like I had two heads.

"Why would I send you away, *mi alma*? You're my soul, my whole world."

I wiped at my face with the backs of my hands, trying to clear the tears without smearing blood on my face. "But I made you do this…" I waved my hand at what was left of my stalker. "You sounded so upset afterward. How can you forgive me for forcing you to do something that caused you pain?"

He huffed out a laugh and started back toward the manor. "Your mind takes you to strange places sometimes. I am a monster, Lisa. Going into a killing rage is part of who I am, and I'll gladly do it every day of the rest of my life if that's what is required to keep you safe. I was upset, to use your word, over what that bastard had done to you in the past. That I hadn't found you sooner to prevent you from being hurt."

Unsure what to say to that, I cuddled in against him, ignoring the coppery stench of blood that now covered us both. He strode through the front door but paused when he reached Henry, who'd barked out a curse as we'd entered.

"Master Noah, I tried to stop her from following. Where is she hurt? What do you need?"

"No need to worry, Henry, we all know how stubborn my little Lisa is. And she's unharmed. The blood is not hers or mine. There is a mess out in the woods that needs tending to, though. Not sure we can pass it off as an animal attack without inciting a massive hunt for said animal. A fire might be a better option. If that's needed, I'll handle it later, after I get Lisa cleaned up and settled."

As soon as Noah finished speaking, he strode off toward our wing. Closing my eyes, I rested my forehead against his neck, trying to calm my racing heart and thoughts.

Once in the bathroom, it only took him a few moments to have the water sorted and us under the warm spray. Lowering me to my feet, he set about gently washing every inch of my body before he got to work on his own. He'd shrunk back down to his normal height, which was still over seven feet. His nails were no longer claws and his teeth were human-looking again. It was odd how he had so many different forms.

"You're very quiet, *mascota*. What's wrong?"

"It's nothing. I'm just thinking. Processing."

He frowned down at me like he didn't believe me. I wasn't sure how to voice everything I was feeling after what had just happened, especially when I added in what I'd been thinking about before Christopher arrived. Outside, he'd said I was his life, indicated he wouldn't send me away. But now he'd calmed down, was that still the case? And for how long? Just until he got his fill? How long would that take?

"Did my true monster form scare you? Do you not want me anymore?"

He flipped off the water and guided me out to the mat where he started drying me off with a big, fluffy towel.

"You were covered in blood, and I still happily clung to you, Noah. I think it's safe to say your monster form didn't scare me."

He frowned as he finished drying me then himself. Once he was done, I lifted my hand and started to run my fingers over his chest. Between the dim lighting and my lack of glasses, I could barely make out the dark lines of his veins. When I didn't say anything else, he took my chin gently between his thumb and finger and tilted my face up until I had to look him in the eyes. His dark gaze glittered while he stared into my face as though he could somehow see what I wouldn't say if he just tried hard enough.

"What is it, then? Are you planning on leaving now you're safe?"

Tears stung my eyes as a sigh left me. I needed to explain what I'd realized in the library earlier today. Hopefully, he really did feel the same way and we could move forward on more solid ground. If not, well, it was better to know now rather than later, right? He moved his palm to cup my face, wiping under my eye with his thumb, catching tears.

"Before Christopher came barging in, I was thinking how I was nearly done cataloging the library. That maybe I shouldn't have worked so quickly because I'd need to leave soon. And I didn't know how you really felt for me. Like, do you take on human women pets often? Am I just one of many and a face that'll blend into the others after I'm gone? Then he came and everything happened. You said I was your whole world. But for how long?"

With my heart on the verge of shattering into a million pieces, my tears kept flowing, too many for him to keep wiping them all away. They trailed down my cheeks, dropping on my breasts as he held my face up and kept his gaze locked onto mine.

"So, you're saying you want to stay indefinitely? Here, with me."

I nodded as much as I could in his grip, and he relaxed, loosening his hold on me.

"I'd been having similar thoughts, but I wasn't sure how you felt about me either. You have a high sex drive, and I can satisfy that, but is that all I am to you?"

I flicked my finger over one of his nipples and grinned through my tears at him, trying to lighten the moment. "You understand there are some really great toys on the market now, right? While no other man has ever been able to keep up with my needs, I had several battery-operated boyfriends that handled the job just fine. I could always buy more." Growing serious again, I pressed myself up against his front. "As great as the sex is, that's not why I want to stay. Well, it's not the only reason."

His hand dropped from my face to rest on my shoulder, where he started playing with the ends of my wet hair. With a deep breath, I rubbed my palms over my face, wiping the tears away. I couldn't do this in a bathroom.

"Let's go sit down."

With one of his large hands on my lower back, he guided me out to the bedroom.

"Wait here, I'll be right back."

With a frown, I watched as he vanished into his ghost form. Where the hell was he going? With a shake of my head, I grabbed the throw blanket from the back of the lounge and wrapped it around myself before I sat down and stared into the crackling flames of the fire.

My mind flicked back to the section of the library I'd been working on this morning. Folklore and fairytale books. Remembering those tales, my breath caught as other thoughts filled my mind. Noah was a supernatural. All those old tales had to start somewhere, right?

I jerked in surprise when I was suddenly lifted but calmed when I found myself on Noah's lap. Now back in his monster form, he held my glasses out for me.

"Oh, thank you." Taking them from him, I used the edge of the blanket to clean them before putting them back on. Now I had him here to keep me warm, I shed the blanket and moved to straddle his lap but kept my calves resting along each of his large thighs, so I wasn't tempted to take his thick cock inside me just yet. Lifting up on my knees, I rested my hands on his shoulders so I could look directly into his face. He raised an eyebrow in question as his hands came to rest on my hips, his thumbs stroking the tender skin near my hip bones.

I got straight to the point. "In the bathroom earlier, were you trying to get me to tell you how I feel in order to break your curse? If I declare my love, will you turn into some sort of Prince Charming?"

His lips quirked as though he was trying really hard not to laugh. Then all humor fled his expression, and he tilted his head to the side.

"Is that what you want? Me to turn into

a human male, someone you can proudly show off in town?"

I growled at him as I tried to shake his shoulders, not that he moved even a fraction of an inch. How could he even think that! "If that's what will happen when I declare my feelings, I will *never* breathe a word of how I feel about you because I want my ghost monster who cherishes me and pampers me. Who will gently dry my tears when I have moments of insanity where I question everything around me. Who will tear to shreds anyone who dares to lay a finger on me." I blew out a breath. "Not even my own parents wanted me. I was abandoned at a damn fire station as a newborn. None of the foster families wanted to keep me. I have no one out in the world who I care about enough to want to impress. I think, for the first time in my life, I'm happy right where I am. And I don't want to do anything that might risk that."

I was breathing heavily by the time I finished my rant. At some point as I'd spoken, he tightened his grip on me and he now wore a wide grin.

"You done?"

Heat raced over my cheeks, and I ducked my gaze from his. Embarrassed, I tried to shift off his lap, but he kept me where I was.

"Um, yeah. I'm done. For now."

NOAH

I could barely hold in my joy and relief at her lecture. She'd been worried I was trying to use her to break a curse or some shit. Had basically told me she loved me in her little rant. Which was good, because the woman was my whole damn world.

I'd feared the worst when I returned from fetching her glasses and she'd been so deep in thought and not looking happy about whatever it was her mind had come up with. I needed to talk to her about what I'd learned from the twins earlier but wanted her to be comfortable and able to see how serious I was, so I'd risked taking a few minutes to go get her glasses.

"What if we could make things between us permanent?"

She tilted her head and frowned at me. "What do you mean?"

"Well, I've been busy with a little research project lately and I finally found the information I was searching for earlier today. The witch who my father employed put in some extra clauses above and beyond what my father had requested of her. She gave us the ability to take a mate, to bind her to us." I paused to clear my throat. "Forever."

She lowered down, her ass coming to rest on her calves. The movement caused her hands to slip from my shoulders to resting on her thighs, and I instantly missed the contact. Needing to touch her, I trailed my fingers over the outside of her thighs and hips, keeping it non-sexual for the moment. I could see her lush tits along with her sweet little pussy and part of me wanted nothing more than to pull her forward until I could sink deeply into her, but this conversation was too important. If she agreed, I'd be able to fuck her for the rest of my days.

"How many mates have you had?"

I fought not to smile. She was so precious, getting jealous that she may not be the only one for me. Leaning in, I pressed a quick kiss to her lips before pulling back. "None. I'm immortal, pet. If you agree to mating me, you'll live as long as I do. Forever by my side. I'll never take another."

She was wringing her hands together as she processed what I was saying. I hated she was nervous about this, and I wished I could simply make the decision for her and claim her, but I couldn't. Not on something that was this important. I needed her to choose me on her own.

"And a family?"

I chuckled. "We'll never be rid of my siblings, especially the twins and Cole. They liked you before today, but now that you've shown them your inner warrior woman, they'll be in your face." I gave her a wink before I continued, "If you mean children, we can have as many as you like. Once we're mated, you'll be able to get pregnant."

She huffed out a chuckle. "And I guess that's why you've never asked me about birth control. I'm on it, by the way."

I shrugged, doubting any drugs in her system would survive the magic that would flow between us when we mated, but I wasn't going to bring that up right now.

She suddenly looked up at me with a glare. "What do you mean, the twins and Cole already like me? I never met them before today."

I could see she already knew the answer, just like I could see she wasn't going to like my confirming it. I took a deep breath before I responded.

"As you've no doubt guessed, they have a ghost form like me. And, yes, all three of them have been curious enough about you to come check you out."

"While we were *together*?" The last word was in a tone that made it clear she meant when I'd had my cock deep inside her.

I smirked as I flipped my tail up to slap lightly across her ass. "Considering how much time we spend fucking all over the house, yeah."

A blush flared over her cheeks as she sputtered for a moment. Unable to resist, I leaned in and took her mouth again, kissing her deeply until she began to relax. Shifting my hand between her thighs, I began to toy with her pussy, playing in the moisture already soaking her curls, teasing her clit. Pulling from the kiss, I slipped two fingers inside her, twisting until I had her g-spot lined up.

"What do you say, my sweet Lisa? Will you be my mate? Love me forever?"

With a groan, she rose up onto her knees again, leaning forward against me so she could kiss me this time. I added a third finger to her pussy, finger fucking her slow and steady while I waited for her response.

With a shuddering breath, she broke the kiss and whispered the sweetest words I've ever heard.

"Yes, Noah. I want to be yours forever. My insatiable ghost monster."

Nudging her knees until they slipped to the outside of my thighs so she was now straddling me, I pulled her forward until I could slide her down my cock.

"Lean back, hands on my knees."

She followed my directions, and I took in the sight she made with her back arched and her tits thrust up to the ceiling. Leaning forward, I took one tip between my lips and sucked until she tensed, then moved over to the other nipple to give it equal treatment. Then I was sitting back in the chair, gripping her hips and getting serious about fucking my beautiful, soon-to-be-mate.

Pressing my thumb over her clit, I pumped my cock into her in a steady rhythm. My free hand moved up to grip her right tit, kneading the large, fleshy globe before I grabbed her nipple and gave it a pinch then twist. She shuddered then shifted her hips, like she wanted me to speed up. Instead of giving in to her silent demands, I grabbed her other nipple and gave that one a rough twist too.

"You don't want to know what mating involves?"

With a groan and frown, she muttered, "I was going to ask then you started fucking me and I forgot."

"I do love how easily I can distract you, *mascota*."

I proved the point with a harder thrust, going deep enough to tap her cervix the way she liked before returning to shallower movements.

Panting, she tried to speak again. "What does the mating involve?"

Leaning over her arched body, I wrapped my mouth around the tip of her right breast and bit down hard enough to break skin. I sucked a small mouthful of blood before I pulled away without licking the wounds shut.

"Blood, sex, cum and magic."

Moving over to her left tit, I did the same thing, circling her nipple with a bite that welled with blood when I left it. She shuddered as the pain mixed with her pleasure. Running my hands up under her spine, I stood and carried her over to the bed, laying her flat on the soft black sheets so I could fuck her hard and fast.

"Come. Closer." Her words were broken by my thrusts but when she reached toward my face, I leaned over her, curious at what she had in mind as I continued to rub over every nerve I could inside her pussy with my every stroke.

She grabbed my horns as soon as I was in range, twisting her palms around them and sending stars across my vision. "Fuck. So good."

Lowering down, I licked at the blood now dripping down her tits, being careful not to seal the still bleeding wounds. Technically, I only needed to bite her once as she came, but fuck that. I wanted her marked all over.

Lifting away from her slightly, I released her hips and got my hands on her nipples, twisting and tugging them, smearing her blood over her pale skin. Her grip tightened on my horns as she wrapped her legs around my waist the best she could, digging her heels into my ass. She was close. In just a few moments, she'd be bound to me forever.

Planting a palm on the mattress above each of her shoulders, I ground down into her, making sure I stroked her g-spot before slamming against her cervix, and then she was arching under me as she screamed and came.

Her orgasm had her channel rippling around my cock, bringing me to the brink of climaxing myself. Lowering my mouth to the ball of her shoulder, I sank my teeth into her again. This time when I took her blood into my mouth, it sang through my system, quickly flowing through my whole body.

The mating magic at work, tying me to her and her to me. Joy sung through my blood as I continued with the ritual.

CHAPTER
NINE

LISA

THE FEEL of him drinking my blood had me coming again. This wasn't the first time he'd bitten me during sex, but previously he'd always sealed the wound straight away. Apparently, mating was messy because I had blood smeared all over my chest, and now he'd bitten into my shoulder too.

His large palm slipped under my head, and he lifted me until my face was pressed in against the tender skin where his shoulder and neck met.

"Bite. Drink of me."

Oh, fuck, he wanted me to drink his blood?

He growled, "Now, Lisa. Or the bond

won't be complete. If you want me—our mating—you need to do this now."

That had me pushing aside the eww factor and I nuzzled in against the soft skin, giving it a lick before I took a small amount of his hot skin between my teeth and bit down as hard as I could to try to break through with my blunt human teeth. He had sharp monster teeth he could call on to get this job done. So unfair.

Then, a taste like I'd never experienced flooded my mouth. It was hot enough that it almost scalded my tongue, but it didn't have the coppery taste I'd been expecting. It was fruity, like a ripe Pomegranate, but different. With a moan, I sucked down another mouthful. It was addictive and I could drink him down all day.

"Enough, *mi alma*. There's one more step."

Reluctantly, I released his neck and he gently lowered me so I was laying against the bed again. Gripping my hips, he pulled his pelvis back, causing me to wince as his huge cock slipped free of me. No matter how many times he fucked me, his size was always enough to leave an ache. One I loved.

He stroked his palm over my pussy, gathering our combined cum in his hand before he smeared it over my shoulder, over the bite. A tingling sensation started immediately. Sparks traveled under my skin, through my blood stream, changing me. I was barely aware when he returned to my pussy, this time filling both palms before he smeared it over my breasts, rubbing our cum into my skin, and sending more sparks flying through me.

"Your turn, *mi alma*."

When I didn't move because I couldn't do a damn thing other than pant through whatever was happening to me, he wrapped his palm around my wrist, then ran my hand between my thighs before he pressed my cum-slickened palm over my bite on him.

The moment he did, power jolted through my hand, adding to the buzzing already going on inside me. Pleasure and pain mixed until the pain won and stole my breath. Opening my mouth, I silently screamed as my body started to convulse while I struggled to suck in enough air. My vision dimmed for a moment, then returned to reveal the outline of two identical men — or monsters — standing beside the table.

"Twins—"

Before I could finish my question, my vision dimmed again and my body gave out, sending me into a blissful darkness where the pain was finally gone.

NOAH

Panicked, I looked over to the twins who had come closer as Lisa's body had started convulsing.

"She could see us?"

I frowned as I snapped out of my shock and reached to check her neck for a pulse. "That's the least of my concerns."

It took me a moment, but when a steady beat thrummed against my fingertips, I slumped over her body with relief, pressing soft kisses over her face. She was alive.

For a few moments, horror had overtaken me as I thought I'd killed my love. Sliding my arms under her limp body, I gathered her up against my chest and ignoring the twins and their questions, strode toward the bathroom. I shifted my grip so I could get the bath started without having to put her down. It was going to be a while before I'd risk letting her out of my sight. Thinking she'd died was not something I was going to get over quickly.

Once the tub was filled, I climbed in, keeping her tucked against me. Once in, I moved her so her head was against my shoulder, well away from the surface of the water. Curled on her side against me, I ran my hands over her body, watching as the blood and cum floated away from her skin, revealing the sealed scars of my marks. While I could only see some of her tits, it was enough to see bits of my round bite marks. The sight of them had my cock twitching and coming back to life. Rubbing my chin over her hair, I sighed and tried to relax. I hoped that when she woke, she wasn't in any pain. Watching her writhe in agony had shattered my heart into pieces.

I never wanted to hurt her, to cause her pain that didn't just heighten her pleasure. To be the one who caused her enough agony that she would convulse before passing out tore at my soul.

With a small moan, she wriggled against me, her palm sliding over my chest until it rested over my heart. I placed my hand over hers, stroking along her fingers.

Keeping my voice low so not to startle her, I spoke, "Are you feeling well?"

"Better."

She pressed a kiss to her mark on me and I hissed as sparks fired through my bloodstream until they reached my cock, which pulsed and jerked with arousal. She stilled but I rubbed a hand down her back and over her ass until she relaxed again.

"You scared me, *mi alma*."

She rolled to her front, her legs slipping to either side of my waist as she pressed her palms against my shoulders so she could sit back. Her pussy rubbed over the underside of my cock as she sank to sit on my lap.

"Not as scared as me. I thought I was going to blow apart into a million pieces."

She started to rock against me, sliding her slick — and not from the bathwater — pussy up and down my length.

"What does *mi alma* mean?"

"A Spanish endearment, reserved for use only with someone we love a great deal."

"Oh. You love me?"

I nodded my head with a grin at her teasing.

"Yes, mate, I love you more than life itself."

Her smile widened and she leaned in to kiss me lightly on the lips before pulling back.

"That's good to hear, *mate*, because I love you too."

Unable to resist my need for her a moment longer, I lifted her up until my cock lined up with her entrance, then lowered her back down on one long stroke until I bottomed out. She arched her back as she slid up my cock, shoving her lush tits near my face before she pushed back down, riding me like the goddess she was.

Releasing her hips to allow her to set the pace, I reached for her tits, running my fingers over my bite marks. Her rhythm faltered and her mouth dropped open. Hmm, those marks were going to be fun. Her nipples were already hard little points, and I grabbed onto them, giving them each a tug and twist as she started to circle her hips over my cock.

"So perfect. *Mi alma.* My mate."

With hooded eyes and flushed cheeks, she moved one of her hands up to rub over my horns, tearing a groan from me that echoed around the bathroom. Slipping my tail up between her cheeks, I teased her ass hole with the tip before entering her. She rocked over me faster as I thickened my tail and started to pump into her ass in the same cadence she was fucking my cock into her pussy.

Water sloshed and hit the tile around the tub, but I didn't give a fuck. My woman—my mate—was not only alive and well but riding me. The world could be crashing and burning around us, and I wouldn't care one bit.

Sliding my hands around her ribs to her slick back, I pulled her toward me until I could take her mouth with mine, kissing her deeply, plunging my tongue between her lips as I took over control of the thrusts into her pussy, lifting my hips each time I drove into her until I was slamming her cervix while my tail fucked deep into her ass.

She gripped both of my horns in her hands as she whimpered against my lips, her body vibrating on the edge of coming. Sucking her tongue into my mouth, I got my hands between our bodies so I could torture her nipples again and that was enough to send her over the edge. Climaxing, she pulled away from the kiss to scream out her pleasure, shaking over me as I continued to fuck her through her high. Just as she was coming down, my own orgasm hit. The first spurt of cum inside her set her off again and my eyes crossed at the pleasure of her walls rippling around me while I came, filling her womb with my seed.

I really hoped the magic of the mating wiped out her birth control. Suddenly, I was desperate to get her pregnant, to see her body swell with my child within her.

With a contented sigh, she slumped against me, and I started to stroke my palms over her back, down over her ass then back up to her shoulders again. I slipped my tail from her body but kept my still hard cock deep in her pussy. I'd live inside her if I could work out how to manage it.

CHAPTER
TEN

LISA

IN THE THREE months since Noah had taken care of my stalker and we'd completed our mating, life sure had been interesting. Especially since bonding with Noah gave me the ability to see monsters when they were in their ghost forms. Not clearly, but I could see their ghostly silhouettes and sense if they were near me. It meant they couldn't sneak around the manor and spy on me anymore. Once they figured that out, they just openly stalked me around the house, clearly curious about me and what it meant for them that their brother had bonded to a mate successfully.

I was still a little embarrassed around the

twins, since they'd been there when Noah had mated me. I'd seen them standing beside us before I'd passed out.

All of the ghost monsters could use some lessons on privacy, but I'd quickly given up trying to change them on that front. They'd simply spent way too long being able to ghost in and out of any place they wanted without consequence to alter their ways now.

Pressing a hand to my belly, I glared at the plastic stick in my other hand.

"Are you well? What's wrong?"

Noah's voice was near panic as he brushed aside my hand to take over rubbing his large palms over my stomach. Another side effect of the mating was he was even more aware of my emotions now. Not always useful.

He took the stick from my hand and looked at it. "What's this?"

"Pregnancy test. Two lines means a positive result."

And there were two very distinct lines on that thing. Of course, after not having a period for three months, I was already fairly sure of the answer, but the mating could have screwed with my cycle so I hadn't been one hundred percent. Not until now.

He stilled for a minute, and I began to panic he didn't want this, then he tipped his head back and let out a whoop before he scooped me up and spun me around. A prickle went up my spine as he stood me back on my feet.

"Get out of our bathroom, dammit! I'm naked!"

With a laugh, Noah set me back on my feet and turned me to face the row of his siblings, all in ghost form who'd come running at his yell. I wrapped an arm over my breasts and put my other hand over the juncture of my thighs as I growled at them all.

Cole waved a hand my way. "Little sister, we've all seen you naked, many times. I'm not sure why you're still bothered by nudity. None of us even own clothes."

That was the truth. I'd never once seen Noah wear clothing of any sort, and I knew he'd prefer it if I gave up wearing them too. Even after all this time, he still liked to fuck me several times a day, whenever and wherever the mood struck him. Not that I was complaining, I loved how insatiable he was. I was equally enthralled with him.

"She's pregnant! My young grows inside her." His palms cupped my soft belly, and I could feel the stares of his strangely silent siblings focused on me. Then the shock wore off and they all started talking at once. I managed to wriggle out of Noah's grasp and move to stand behind him, hiding my body from his insane family.

"Please, make them go away already!"

He chuckled while his tail wrapped around my waist, holding me to him.

"Brothers, leave us. We'll be down in the dining hall later. For now, I want to celebrate with my mate."

After several comments about him not needing to *celebrate* because I was already pregnant, they finally left the room and I slumped against him, resting my forehead against his spine as I ran my palm over his tail that was around my tummy.

"Noah, we really need to work on boundaries with them."

He laughed and turned to face me. "You know that'll never happen. We're ghosts, with the ability to float through walls and doors. We're used to being able to go anywhere we please. It'll be easier for you to learn how to ignore them when you don't want to interact with them."

I shook my head but smiled. He was right. Then another thought hit me.

"What will the baby be? Like you or like me?"

He cocked his head, "Does it matter? We will all love him or her, no matter what they are."

My heart melted at his words and my eyes filled with tears.

"I love you, so much." I drew in a breath and wiped my eyes. "Although, we will need to find a doctor who can be bribed to take care of me. If we have an ultrasound that reveals a tail, things could get ugly for us, and especially for the baby."

He nodded, his expression turning serious. "We'll start looking for a suitable doctor, maybe a midwife. Perhaps we can find a female who will fall for one of my brothers, then she'll be more inclined to keep our secrets safe."

I chuckled at that thought. "You going to

set up a matchmaking service for your siblings now?"

He leaned down to press kisses over his mark on my shoulder, making me shudder as arousal wound through my body, leaving my pussy throbbing with want.

"Just think… if we get all of them paired off, they'll be too preoccupied with their own lives to come interfere with ours."

"That actually has some merit—"

Before I could say more, he lifted me then lowered me over his erection. Wrapping my legs around his waist, I gripped his biceps and arched my back as he went deep, but he stopped short of hitting my cervix and I whimpered. I loved how it felt when he added that little bite of pain to our sex.

"Sorry, *mi alma*, but I'll not risk the baby's safety by touching you so deeply while you're pregnant."

I pouted in disappointment, although my heart swelled at his care and consideration of me and our child. He was the perfect mix of rough and tender and I couldn't love him or our lives together more.

"I love you, Noah."

With a grin, he thrust into me again and lowered his lips to take mine for a deep, passionate kiss that left me breathless.

"You're my world, Lisa. My mate, my love."

NOAH

Later that night, I hovered over the bed in ghost form as my mate slept peacefully.

My *pregnant* mate.

I was going to be a father in another six months, assuming she'd fallen pregnant the night of our mating and followed a standard human pregnancy. Pride filled me that we were going to have a family, but a little fear crept in around the edges. What if something happened to her with the pregnancy? What if the baby was a monster like me, with horns? I shuddered at the thought of my love having to birth such a creature.

"Noah, come to bed."

Her sleepy voice pulled me out of my spiraling thoughts. I stayed hovering in ghost form until she sighed and moved to sit up against the headboard.

"I can feel your fear. How about we just buy our own ultrasound machine so we can keep an eye on how the baby is forming regularly? If there's horns, then we'll sort out a C-section, because trust me, I do not want to push out a baby that has horns. But it'll be okay. Trust that the fates wouldn't have put us together, allow us to mate and get pregnant in the first place if our DNA wasn't a good mix."

I nodded, mollified a little at her logic. "Okay. I'm calming down. I'm just so fucking scared of losing you, it's hard to see past that."

She laughed quietly. "I'm as immortal as you are now, remember? Me dying should be the very least of your concerns."

I growled. "You nearly died during our mating. It will be years, maybe decades before I get over that. Until then, I'll worry."

She gave me a cheeky smile. "Well, how about you come down here and let me do something to ease that worry?"

She leaned out and grabbed my cock, which instantly hardened for her. That was another development with the mating. Not only could she now see me in my ghost form, but she could also touch me without me needing to make it so she could. Tightening her grip, she pulled me forward, my body floating over until I was hovering right in front of her. She didn't stop until she had my cock at her lips, which she rubbed over the tip before she lapped up the drops of precum that leaked from the head.

With a hum, she opened wide and took me deeply to the back of her throat and my mind emptied of every worry I had. Pleasure buzzed through me as she hummed while she deep throated my cock like a pro.

"Fuck. So good."

I wrapped my hands in her hair and guided her movements as she continued to send me to paradise with her wicked mouth and tongue. My tail slipped down and when the tip slid up the inside of her thigh, she spread her legs wide, giving me plenty of room to use my tail to play with her pussy and clit before thrusting it inside her to stroke her inner walls, making sure to focus in on her g-spot. Before I could utter the words, her hands came up to tease and torture her lush tits and nipples.

There hadn't been a single day since she'd come to the manor where I haven't fucked her several times a day. She was as insatiable as I was, and after the mating, her stamina had increased so we could go even longer with our sex marathons, especially once she'd finished cataloging the library. That had freed up her time considerably, and I put that time to good use until she demanded that she needed something to do with her days. That had led to her working with Henry on getting better internet service set up in the manor, and she now spent hours each day in the library, searching online for rare books to add to our collection. I often helped her. I hadn't ever worried about learning the internet before, but now that Lisa had taught me how useful it was, I loved it. I even had my own laptop here in our room to use when I couldn't sleep.

I only needed a couple hours of sleep a day, while Lisa still had a normal human sleep cycle of resting all night. Well, almost all night. I generally fucked her at least twice during those dark hours. Sometimes, I'd stay in my ghost form and not even wake her as I slowly made love to her.

There was never a dull moment in my life now I had my mate, and with a baby on the way, I knew life was only going to get better for us both.

I couldn't wait.

Thank you so much for reading Insatiable Ghost Monster. I hope you enjoyed reading Noah and Lisa's story as much as I did writing it.

If you have a few spare minutes, I'd love it if you could tell others what you thought of Insatiable Ghost Monster by leaving a review online.

If you'd like to know when more Ghost Monster books, or any of my other new releases, will come out, or where you can see me in person, follow the link below to sign up for my newsletter.
newsletter.khloewren.com/ghost1

Keep reading for a teaser from book 2,
Ravenous Ghost Monster,
Cole and Katherine's story.

KATHERINE

The car pulling to a stop had me jerking me out of my thoughts and with a shake of my head, I grabbed my bag. Before I could open the door, Henry was there doing it for me.

"Thanks, Henry."

"You're most welcome, Miss Turner. I look forward to seeing you soon."

With a smile, I waved before turning to walk toward my apartment building. Once through the door, I nearly ran up the stairs and down the hallway with all the excitement I had running through my veins. Once inside, I looked around the living area of my one-bedroom apartment. I'd told Lisa I needed a month, but I doubted I'd last that long. This place was a dump and even if it wasn't, I doubted anything could compare to the manor house. I hadn't seen a bedroom, but I could imagine how luxurious they would be.

Maybe I should have agreed to move straight in, but that seemed like a dangerous thing to agree to so quickly. I needed to play it cool, not act like I was raised in a commune by an overprotective mother and a bunch of other people who were equally paranoid about the outside world. William had done a fabulous job setting up the retreat for anyone who'd suffered abuse. Many women came there pregnant or with young children with nothing but the clothes on their backs. They were always welcome, and a home was made for them. But they understandably didn't want to leave to give birth.

Guilt ate at me again for even thinking about not going back. But I didn't need those high fences to make me feel safe. As I'd grown older, they'd felt more suffocating than secure. A vision of Ash's smirking face had a shudder running through me. Sometimes, it seemed like genetics were stronger than upbringing. Ash's father was a bastard who'd beaten his mother to the point she had a miscarriage. His mom was the sweetest woman, but Ash was more like his father, possessive with a mean streak. He'd not been subtle in letting me know he considered me his. Just like I'd been equally clear in letting him know no man would ever own me. I'd made the mistake of sleeping with him once, but I had no intention of repeating that mistake. Thankfully, he knew if he forced himself on me, he would get kicked out of the retreat. William had a zero-tolerance policy on that type of behavior.

Needing to clear my mind, I went to my bedroom and stripped out of my clothes, tossing them into my laundry basket. In nothing but panties, I pulled out my dresser drawers for my workout clothes. Pulling on my sports bra, I had my arms stretched up and the fabric over my face when tingles spread over both my breasts, just like back at the manor. With a gasp, I pulled the bra back off and tossed it aside before looking in the mirror. Something was definitely touching me, cupping my boobs and lifting them. It was damn surreal to see the girls moving without anything touching them.

Ghosts, indeed.

"Guess you followed me from Gallichan Manor, huh?"

Warmth engulfed the tip of my right breast, and a shiver ran down my spine when the other nipple was pinched and twisted.

"Ghost with a boob fetish. My lucky day."

Heat pooled low in my belly as the ghost continued to work my breasts with its mouth and fingers. My gaze stayed glued to the mirror, on how red my nipples were getting, I started to rub my thighs together.

"So, ghostie, you a boy or a girl?"

I was honestly horny enough I didn't really care, but damn, I was hoping it was a male ghost because I could use a dick right about now. I'd always had a high libido, but mostly dealt with it myself. It wasn't like there was a heap of options at the retreat, and those options were often like Ash, thinking he owned a girl if she opened her legs to him. But I'd watched enough TV to know that wasn't how the rest of the world worked. It might be nice to give my dildo a break for one night.

"My name is Colc, not ghostie."

His deep voice rumbled over my nerves.

"Boy ghost then. Good."

Something warm and slick covered the tip of each breast a moment before a gentle suction tugged on both my nipples. With a gasp, I threw out an arm to press my hand against the wall. I had no fucking idea how he'd managed to do what he was doing, but I never wanted him to stop.

"You are not afraid that I'm a ghost?"

I shook my head. "Ghosts fascinate me. Never actually met one before, and didn't realize they could…" My voice trailed off as my panties started to slide over my hips and down my legs until they dropped to the floor around my feet.

"Put your back against the wall, then spread your legs."

His voice was low, so compelling, that almost before I could process the request, I was moving, pressing my spine against the smooth wall as I lifted each foot out of my underwear before moving them to shoulder width apart.

To read the full story follow the link below:

www.books2read.com/ RavenousGhostMonster

RAVENOUS GHOST MONSTER

Gallichan Manor Series Book 2

Blurb:

After being raised by my mother within the walls of a retreat for domestic abuse victims, I am more than ready to spread my wings and experience all life can offer.

A perfectly timed job offer at Gallichan Manor gives me the excuse I was looking for to try living outside of the retreat. But a job isn't the only thing I find when I get to the manor.

My new boss's home is haunted with a ravenous ghost monster who is fixated on me, and it's not long before I'm willingly falling into his tentacles every chance I get.

But my darkly ever after seems suddenly out of reach when I'm kidnapped and held hostage. But I'm not as alone as my captor believes, as my ghost monster comes charging to the rescue.

'Ravenous Ghost Monster' is the adult Beauty and the Beast re-telling you didn't know you needed. Download your copy today and be swept away by this dark, ghostly romance!

For more details head to:

www.books2read.com/ RavenousGhostMonster

BIOGRAPHY

Khloe Wren lives in rural South Australia with her husband, two daughters and an ever changing list of animals!

She started writing in 2013 and has published over 50 books since then in the romantic suspense genre. She writes both paranormal and contemporary stories, including her best selling series Charon MC.

Khloe enjoys writing outside of the box and she loves her heroes strong, and her heroines even stronger.

f facebook.com/khloe.wren.3

⊙ instagram.com/khloewren

BB bookbub.com/authors/khloewren